GRAVE
CONSEQUENCES

By the Author

Jade Murphy Diaries Series:

Racing the Dawn

Blood Memory

Dark Truths

Grave Consequences

Visit us at www.boldstrokesbooks.com

GRAVE
CONSEQUENCES

by

Sandra Barret

2023

GRAVE CONSEQUENCES

ISBN 13: 978-1-63555-467-9

This Trade Paperback Original Is Published By
Bold Strokes Books, Inc.
P.O. Box 249
Valley Falls, NY 12185

First Edition: December 2023

Credits
Editor: Shelley Thrasher
Production Design: Stacia Seaman
Cover Design by Tammy Seidick

Acknowledgments

Thank you to my editor, Shelley Thrasher, for her help massaging drafts into a cohesive story. Gratitude to all the fine folks at Bold Strokes Books who make being an author so enjoyable.

As always, thanks to my wife, who puts up with my harebrained ideas and helps me morph them into something people might actually want to read.

And thank you to the readers, who make this all worthwhile!

To Ma—you're gone in body but with us in spirit, forever.

CHAPTER ONE

Tamar, have you checked on Room 203?"

Tamar Richler looked up from the nursing station computer, did a quick mental translation, and nodded to her boss. "Yes. Mr. Melnyk's vitals are fading. His daughter is on her way."

Tamar loved her boss, sometimes a bit too much, but she was annoyed at the woman's tendency to report on their hospice patients as room numbers instead of individuals. Tamar took the effort to memorize each one's name and family information as they came into hospice at the Sunlight Hospice Care facility, where she worked.

Her boss looked back at Tamar. "It must be over an hour drive up here from Boston. Think she'll make it on time?"

"I know she will."

Her boss gave her a sad smile. "I don't know how you manage to predict these situations, but you're right most of the time."

Tamar hid her blush by staring back at her computer screen. She knew exactly how she did it, but it was sort of illegal. She didn't give the patients extra drugs. She gave them extra life. Tamar Richler was an untrained, unlicensed necromancer. A resurrector, according to Professor Google and her online searches. She'd never tried a real resurrection, but since getting her nursing license and becoming a hospice nurse, she'd learned how to give just a bit of herself to a hospice patient who might be passing before their loved ones could arrive and spend their final moments together.

Her boss put her hand on Tamar's shoulder, a lovely, warm hand that turned Tamar's blush into a full-on burn of embarrassment. Yeah. Tamar had a crush on her boss—a silly, foolish crush, because her boss had a wonderful husband and two teenage kids. Her boss's gate swung only one way, but that didn't stop Tamar's feelings or the heat building in unmentionable places when her boss came near. She was one of the few people shorter than Tamar, coming in at about five feet, with naturally black hair wrapped with a bright-patterned green scarf holding it back in a puff. That was a hairstyle argument her boss had with corporate when she joined the floor two years ago, and she'd won hands down.

"You look exhausted," her boss said. "Why don't you head home? There's only thirty minutes left on your shift. I can cover that."

Yet another reason for Tamar's hopeless crush. Her boss took compassion to a new level sometimes.

"Thanks," Tamar mumbled. Her tired state was a direct result of the partial resurrection she'd just done for Mr. Melnyk so he would still be aware when his daughter came to say good-bye. Tamar wrapped up her data entry and headed out the door. The late-afternoon sun peeked out from a bank of clouds as a warm September breeze blew through her unruly curls. She drove her orange Jeep home and unlocked the door to her first-floor apartment. A boundless bundle of energy jumped up and pinned her to the wall with his front paws.

"Okay, okay! You missed me. I get it!" She scratched Kalev, her black Lab, behind the ears and lowered his paws back to the ground. "Now let a girl get inside, okay?"

She knew she'd have to take him out for a walk soon. It had been four hours since her upstairs neighbor had done that. Her neighbor had retired from her job as a teacher five years ago and used Kalev as an excuse both to get some exercise and to guard against anyone who might think about taking advantage of a seventy-year-old woman out on her own in Gloucester, Massachusetts. Not that anyone should be afraid of Kalev. He was seventy-five pounds of cuddle, but would-be muggers wouldn't know that.

First, though, Tamar really needed a short rest. She shuffled into her living room, which faced the front of her building. She had a choice between an upright chair with unyielding, black-and-white-checkered cushions or a dark green sofa with soft throw pillows. It wasn't much of a competition. She loved the chair because it was a gift from her grandmother, who'd raised her since she was seven, but a comfy sofa won out for sure. With the blinds tilted for light but privacy, Tamar peeled off her scrubs and kicked them to the floor. She flopped onto the sofa in her boxers and sports bra and fell asleep while Kalev nudged into his place beside her on the now-cramped sofa.

She woke up an hour later as the low sun angled in. Her energy hadn't returned, which she took as a good sign. Mr. Melnyk must still be alive, or she'd have felt it. Kalev hopped off the sofa and eyed her face-to-face. She knew what he wanted, and maybe she did have the energy for one more excursion today.

Tamar walked to her bedroom at the far side of the apartment and laid a pair of red swim trunks on her queen-sized bed, along with a bikini top and a windbreaker. Kalev gave one quick yip and jumped up on her bed.

"I didn't even say the word yet!" She knew better than to say "beach" in front of her dog, but he obviously recognized the swim clothes and knew he was in for a treat. Dressed for a swim she didn't think she'd have the energy for, Tamar stepped into her kitchen and sat in one of the high chairs, resting her head for a moment on her folded arms on the Formica island. She took a long, slow, breath, trying to convince herself she was ready to let go of Mr. Melnyk. A cantankerous old man, but so well-loved by his family, he must have been a great father and grandfather.

She lifted her head when Kalev put his big head in her lap. "Yes. Yes. I put on the clothes. That's practically a legally binding contract to take you to the beach, isn't it?"

Kalev scrambled past her, grabbed the hanging end of his lead from the wall hook, and tugged at it. He trotted back to her, clearly knowing just how clever he was. Tamar gave him a tired smile and clipped on the lead. Before she left, she grabbed a towel for each of them and snacks. Beaches required snacks. That's something she and her dog agreed on wholeheartedly.

The drive to the beach took less than fifteen minutes. Mid-September saw a dramatic cutback in the number of visitors to Gloucester. Even the locals seemed to give up on beach fun shortly after Labor Day. She preferred these warm days before fall with fewer people and the beaches available to dogs.

"Their loss, our gain," she said to Kalev as she opened the back hatch and let him jump out. He waited just long enough for her to toss him a ball before he ran off along the sandy beach with far more energy than she had.

Tamar followed at a slower pace, her flip-flops kicking up still-warm sand as she found a spot close enough to the shore to keep an eye on her water-loving dog, but far enough away that he'd shake the water out of his coat before coming to bug her for more attention.

She sat in the cooling sand, watching the tide go out. Gloucester in off-season had a beauty not visible with the summer crowds. Midweek meant she had the sunset virtually to herself. She shut her eyes and let the ocean scent and the sound of lapping waves wash away her exhaustion.

That peace and quiet lasted less than a minute, when her black Lab trotted back to her and shook the salty water off his coat.

"Dagnabbit, Kalev!" she said. "Did you have to wait until you were right next to me to do that?" Not that she didn't want to get wet. The ocean remained warm even if the air temperature leaned toward the cooler side. "I'd have liked to get into the water on my own terms, you know."

Kalev dropped his ball at her sandy feet as if that made up for it all.

Tamar grinned, picked it up, and tossed it back into the low surf. Of course it made up for it all. Kalev took off after it.

"'Beware of still water, a still dog, and a still enemy.'" Her grandmother's Jewish quotes never failed to creep back into Tamar's memory, but this one worked. The waves weren't still, her dog was splashing in those waves, and she had no enemies. All to the good!

Tamar peeled off her windbreaker and walked to those waves. Her feet squished into the cool, wet sand, but that didn't prepare her for the first wave that tickled her toes. If she had the energy, she'd get all the way in, but she still felt the exhaustion from work.

It was a good feeling, though. It meant she'd helped her patient the best she knew how. She didn't glance at her smartwatch, but with the angle of the sun on the horizon behind her, she knew his family would be with him for his last moments.

Being a hospice nurse took a lot out of Tamar, but when she could give a little back of herself to make sure families got to say good-bye, it was worth the drain and the exhaustion.

Just as the last rays of sun glinted off the waves, she felt a sudden burst of energy. She looked back at the setting sun, opposite the waves. "Rest in peace," she whispered.

She knew her patient had passed, the way any necromancer knew—the life force that Tamar had given to Mr. Melnyk to help him remain awake in his final moments came back to Tamar in a jolt that some nefarious necromancers called "juicing up." To her it wasn't that. It was a last good-bye.

Tamar turned to the waves and walked in up to her hips before she dove in and let the cool water wash over her and clean away the sorrow. Her energy increased. She floated in the waves with a smile and a dog barking on the surf because he wouldn't get in as deep as she floated.

Chicken, she thought with a grin.

❖

"Dr. Wu, you wanted to know when we had another necromancer volunteer?"

Maddy Wu glanced up from her laptop at her assistant, Devin, standing in the open door of her glass-enclosed office. "Believable story?"

Devin shook his head. "Not to be biased, but sounds like another wannabe necromancer looking for proof of what probably isn't there."

Maddy took off her blue-light-filtering computer glasses and pinched the bridge of her nose. She'd had state approval to start up the first privately funded necromancer testing site for two months now. Two months of providing a free service to help necromancers identify their abilities and qualify for the training and licensing program her brother Kenneth had pushed through the Massachusetts Statehouse.

"With state grants available for the two community colleges offering the new necromancy program, we're bound to attract interest." Even if the accreditations for both were still pending at the federal level. "It's a beginning," she said. A beginning she'd fought for right beside her brother.

"Do you want me to take the blood draw?" Devin asked.

Maddy sighed. "Yes. Prepare it with yesterday's sample, and I'll run both through the standard blood tests myself tonight. Thanks."

"Will do."

Devin stepped out again, and Maddy leaned back in her black office chair to stare out the window. Her view of the sunset sending glowing beams across the blue pond outside their office park did little to lighten her mood. After two months of blood samples and tests, she had a batch of seventy-five blood draws, with only eight that showed signs of actual necromancer ability. The rest of the volunteers told stories of resurrected pets and other tall tales, but she doubted most of those stories. Since the federal government legalized necromancy with controlled and licensed regulations, it had become a popular trope in movies and TV shows. While that helped destigmatize her kind, it also created an undercurrent of normal humans wanting to be something special that dragged on the funding for her projects.

She put her glasses back on and stared at her test results, a call on her cell phone interrupting her a moment later. She smiled as she picked it up. "You always know when I have data, don't you?"

"Hi to you too, Maddy, my girl."

Her brother's voice relaxed some of the tension Maddy held in her shoulders. "Hello, Kenneth. And how's your day been?"

"Wrangling compromises out of state senators, pressing palms with mayors who think necromancy schools are great so long as they aren't in their city. The usual."

"Not in my backyard," she said. "You love it, though."

"Yes. Yes, I do. My little badge does say necromancer marshal on it, after all."

He didn't have an actual badge, except the one he picked up from a toy store the day he was promoted to that position last year. It remained a running joke between them. "How's your data then, since my spidey sense says you have it up."

"Inconclusive," Maddy said. "I'm short another four samples at least before I can run DNA tests on the batch. I still can't isolate which necromancer has the potential to fully resurrect another human based on genetic markers in their blood."

"But you can determine which are from potential necromancers."

Most necromancers had some level of ability for deathbed depositions, where the licensed necromancer could reengage the memories of the departed to provide a court-ordered deposition in cases of presumed wrongful death. Full resurrection remained rare.

"Yes. That's evident from simple blood tests. The volunteers have signed release waivers so I can continue tests on their blood once I have enough, both human and necromancer."

"Now you're channeling our opposition there," he said.

"Channeling what we all grew up with, but you're right. Continuing to use outdated terminology doesn't help our drive for full acceptance. We're all humans."

He chuckled. "Just some of us are better-equipped humans."

Maddy smiled. Kenneth had always had a way of lifting her spirits when they were children. He didn't try as often as he used to, but when he did, it always worked.

"Thanks."

"I have faith in you, little sister," he said. "How about dinner?"

"I can't. I want to run the most recent batch through the blood tests tonight."

"Okay," he said before hanging up. "I know better than to suggest you should just put it off until tomorrow."

Sometimes she wished he would, but he equaled her in drive and motivation to move the necromancy world forward. His talents shone in the political sphere, something Maddy never would have thought, given what he'd been like as a teenager, before the accident. But then neither of them was the same after that, were they?

A ping on her computer brought Maddy out of her reverie. Devin messaged that the blood samples were prepped and ready. Maddy pushed back from her desk and grabbed her cane. She headed to the elevator and back to work.

She tried not to see her own reflection in the elevator doors, but it was hard to avoid. Her straight black hair with the highlights she'd added a month ago remained pulled back in a ponytail at the nape of her neck. Her dark blue dress fell straight, erasing some of the evidence of her weight gain. Presentable after a long day, but her dark brown eyes told a different story. She felt tired, as always. If she didn't pace herself better, she'd be sick by the end of the week. Chronic fatigue and frequent lab work weren't a good combination. Maybe she could work from home tomorrow. After she analyzed these test batches.

Her lab at Conn BioTech had that pristine appearance from pictures—white lab benches covered in expensive equipment with blue metal stools to provide the least amount of comfort possible. Most of her lab associates just stood up, but that wasn't an option for Maddy, so it was uncomfortable stools for her. Someday she'd requisition a better lab chair for herself.

She paused at the prep room outside the lab to pull on a lab coat, gloves, mask, and safety glasses, then proceeded into the lab. She didn't don the equipment all the time, but definitely when she was running blood tests. She walked past the giant DNA analyzer, the company's latest flagship product, the CR-2000. She pressed her palm against it. "Someday, soon, you'll get to work." She needed only four more samples from actual necromancers.

She pulled up a stool next to the sample tray Devin had left for her. The bench included the microscope with touch-screen display that would help her identify necromancers, as well as a laptop to enter the test results into her database.

The first-level necromancy tests were crude but simple. Devin had already labeled three test trays for her—one for each sample and one non-necromancer control. She prepped each tray with the test material, in this case just a milligram of partially decayed plant material. Then she used a fresh pipette to transfer three milliliters of blood from each necromancy sample into the two sample trays, and one sample from the control.

She set a timer for thirty seconds, and when it beeped, she put the control sample under the microscope and studied the display. She adjusted the focus and verified there was no change to the plant sample. Pushing that control tray to the side, she picked up the sample one and repeated the test.

No change. Human normal. She added that fact into the laptop and picked up the last sample, repeating the steps.

She sat up taller, adjusted the display again to focus in on one area of activity. "There you are," she whispered.

The display showed cell-level healing in the plant test material. Necromancer.

One down, three to go.

CHAPTER TWO

Tamar stuffed her head deeper under the pillow but couldn't drown out the sound of her phone ringing on the bedside table. Kalev nudged his wet nose under her arm by the side of the bed.

"Yes. I hear it."

She rolled over and picked up her phone to see who was bugging her at the crack of dawn on a Saturday. She groaned a little louder when she realized the call came from her grandmother and couldn't be ignored. Tamar sat up in bed, ran a hand through her hair just enough to realize it was a lost cause, and accepted the incoming video call.

"Morning, Nanna."

Her grandmother filled the small screen, her brown eyes and wavy hair a reflection of Tamar's, but unlike Tamar's, Nanna's gray hair was pulled back neatly in a wrap.

"Good afternoon, Tamar," Nanna said with an indulgent smile.

Tamar glanced at the time on her phone and winced. "Was a long day yesterday."

"Another of your patients passed?"

"Yes. Mr. Melnyk."

"May his memory be for a blessing."

Tamar nodded in silence to Nanna's traditional expression of sympathy for the family of those who'd passed. Tamar needed to change the topic before Nanna kept on. Her grandmother had a Jewish quote or expression for every occasion, but she also tended to deep-dive into the philosophy behind each one. Seventy-nine years old, and over fifty of those years as a professor of Jewish philosophy in New York, meant she could go on for hours.

"Kalev and I celebrated the Sabbath at the beach yesterday."

"Watching the sun always was your favorite way to start the Sabbath, right along with not getting up until afternoon on the Saturday."

"I'm resting," Tamar said. "Like I'm supposed to."

Nanna laughed. "And you used that excuse all through your teen years as well. Some things never change."

And Nanna's acceptance of her as she was never changed either. Well, mostly. Tamar kept to herself the ways she skirted the rules, both Nanna's rules against necromancy and the state's rules on who could practice it. Some things were best left unsaid and undiscovered on both counts.

"How's the farm?" Tamar asked.

"I lost two chickens last night to a fox. Bennie's coming over tomorrow to see if he can rewire the coop so it doesn't happen again."

Bennie owned the farm next to Nanna's and was the main reason Tamar felt okay moving out after college. Nanna wouldn't be alone so long as Bennie stuck around.

"He's sweet on you, you know?"

Nanna waved a hand. "He's a kind soul. But speaking of that, Rosh Hashana is coming up. You're always welcome to bring a friend along."

Fishing. Nanna loved fishing for details on Tamar's love life. Or her nonexistent love life at the moment. "Thanks, Nanna. It's just me this year."

"You need to get out there more, Tamar. That's why you moved so far from home, isn't it? Because the dating pool in Western Massachusetts was too small for you?"

"More like nonexistent," Tamar said. "But I have a lot of shifts at work. It's hard to meet people."

"People your own age, yes. Don't they have bars out there?"

Tamar took a deep breath. It would be a long discussion now about ways Tamar could find that special someone. No advice landed so well as that coming from a Jewish grandmother!

When the debate over her lack of a love life finally ended the call, Tamar leaned back in bed, hoping to catch a bit more sleep.

The seventy-five pounds of black Lab landing on her bed had other ideas for a cloudy Saturday afternoon. "Sabbath day is for resting, you know."

Kalev slobbered her with dog kisses until she caved. "Okay, okay. I'm getting up."

Tamar pulled on a pair of black shorts and a teal T-shirt and stepped out of her bedroom to see Kalev waiting patiently by the door with his lead in his mouth. "Coffee first," she said and walked to her small kitchen to pull out an individual-serving French press from the fridge. Her cousin had told her at the start of the summer how to make cold-brew coffee by leaving it in the fridge for twenty-four hours, and now that was Tamar's favorite coffee.

She poured the result into a travel mug, clipped Kalev's lead on his collar, and opened the door.

And came face-to-face with Samantha, that same cousin.

"Most people call or text before stopping by," Tamar said.

Samantha leaned down and planted a kiss on Tamar's forehead. "I'm not most people."

That she wasn't. Not at six foot, three inches of bleached-blond, fashion-model gorgeous that turned heads wherever she went. "You're far too perky for a Saturday," Tamar grumbled.

"Love you too, sweetie," Samantha said. "We going for a walk?"

Kalev yipped his excitement because Samantha said the magic word out loud, even though he already had his lead on. He tugged Tamar forward on that lead as she locked the door behind them. "Walk and breakfast," Tamar said.

"Or maybe lunch," Samantha replied.

"Call it what you will, it's my first meal of the day, so… break…fast."

Samantha laughed as they exited the building and led the way down the block toward the food shops. "You're cranky today."

Tamar took a deep, slow breath. "Just got the usual lecture from Nanna."

Samantha gave her the side-eye. "Dating or necromancy?"

Tamar smiled. "Just dating this time. Guess I should count my lucky stars on that one."

"You should just get tested for necromancy. They're offering it for free now over in Beverly. I went last week."

Tamar stopped in her tracks. "You did?" Her heartbeat pounded in her chest. "Did you get the results?"

"One hundred percent human."

Tamar grimaced. "We're all human, Samantha, with or without the necromancer potential."

Samantha nudged her shoulder. "Yes, Nanna."

"She and I don't agree on necromancy, but she does insist on not labeling them something other than human. And I agree with her."

Samantha held up a hand. "You're right. No need to feed into the prejudices already all around us. I see it in my teen clients far too often."

Samantha was a resident expert on teen psychology. She was even once asked in to help the FBI profilers on a particularly heinous teen crime.

"Still," Samantha said, "if you tested and came out negative for necromancy, you'd have one less thing Nanna could nag you about."

Not likely, Tamar thought. Also not likely something she'd

confess to Samantha even if she was Tamar's best friend and family. Again, some things were better left unsaid.

"Nanna will always have something to say about necromancy."

"Right again, cousin. Her generation has some scars, that's for sure. Being forced into a segregated housing estate for those with necromancy in the family left its mark on her." Samantha turned to Tamar. "But that was what, three generations ago? We're in a different world now. Necromancy is even a valid career option for some people. I mean, not our people, of course. Nanna would flip, but still."

"Nanna would also flip if she found out you got tested, especially at that place in Beverly."

"Conn Biotech," Samantha added.

"'First they mark you, and then they eliminate you.'"

"Well, we just won't tell her then, will we?" Samantha said. *Time for a topic change.* "You want breakfast food or any kind of food?" Tamar asked as they walked past what she called church row before turning onto the block with a bunch of coffeehouses and other food options.

"Your choice."

Tamar glanced down the block. "Walt's Sandwiches. They have outdoor seating that accepts dogs."

"Walt's it is," said Samantha. "Then we can talk about your lack of a love life."

Tamar groaned. Not again.

❖

Mornings didn't agree with Maddy, especially mornings when the weather was shifting. She could feel the low-pressure system in her joints as a dull ache that would get worse as the day wore on. She forced herself to sit up in bed and take a few deep breaths before checking her phone for the time.

"Shit," she said, looking at the 2:12 p.m. there. She'd slept half the day away, again. She shifted her legs off the edge of the bed, stuffed her feet into slippers, and stared at her options. Her cane rested by the nightstand and her walker nearer the bathroom. She rolled her ankles a moment and decided the pain wasn't too bad yet. She stood up and walked out of the bedroom without either.

Brighter light illuminated her living room, enhanced by the glass balcony doors that faced out onto the condo's landscaped gardens. She ignored the siren call of her comfortable cream-colored sofa and continued into her chrome-dominated kitchen. It wasn't her favorite type of kitchen decor, but that's what the condo came with, and she hadn't had the energy to change it before she moved in last year. Now she was just used to it.

First stop, coffee. She sat in the high chair by the kitchen island as it brewed, flipping through messages and emails on her phone while she waited. The smell of coffee broke her concentration on work emails. With a fresh cup in one hand and a blueberry muffin in the other, she shifted to the nook next to the kitchen that was meant for a dining table.

Maddy didn't have many guests, so instead of a table, she had a home-office, light-wood desk, complete with dual monitors and a massive desktop computer with more CPU than she really needed. But Conn Biotech insisted she have the best possible home setup, given the number of days she couldn't get into the office due to her chronic condition.

Caffeine filtered into her system as she brought up the latest research paper one of her research assistants had sent her. The title had all the right buzzwords, and the abstract showed promise. Maddy wasn't the only researcher attempting to isolate the necromancy potential, and it helped to keep up on what her peers were publishing.

Three hours later, she hadn't advanced her knowledge any except to realize the potential for bias in some research results that could negatively impact her community. She and Kenneth had a solution for that, if they could ever get it out of committee at the statehouse. Meanwhile, she had other duties for the day.

She took her pet tortoise out of its habitat and placed it on the living-room floor while she cleaned out its shallow water bowl and bedding. Donatello hadn't roamed too far by the time she finished, and she sat on the floor, feeding him some lettuce before placing him back in his habitat. "Maybe next weekend we'll go to a park," she said, knowing she said this every week but hadn't managed to take the tortoise outside in months. Kenneth had bought him, named him, and walked him daily at the family house. He'd lost interest after the accident and left it to her when he went off to college. She'd kept Donatello ever since.

With that done, she called an Uber. She dressed in casual tan slacks and a light-peach blouse, pulling on a rain jacket in case the darkening clouds let loose some much-needed rain, then headed out the door with her cane in one hand, a cooler in the other, and a light backpack with her tablet in it on her shoulders. Her ride took her to the Beverly Small Animal Surgery in ten minutes.

Andre greeted her when she stepped inside the facility. "Glad you're here, Dr. Wu. We have two cats under anesthesia, but one is definitely showing signs of distress before the surgery starts."

Maddy placed the cooler on the plain white counter where Andre stood. "Do you have the signed release form?"

He nodded to her left. "The owner is signing now."

Maddy glanced over to an older woman staring at the fine print on the release form required by the state government to authorize the necromancy tests Maddy was there to administer. She pulled out her lanyard holding her necromancer license ID and picture, walked over, and sat next to the woman.

Maddy held out her hand. "Hello. I'm Dr. Wu. I'll be monitoring your pet's surgery. Is there anything in the form I can clarify for you?" Maddy knew this was the point where half her potential test candidates backed out, and she didn't want to have made this trip on a Saturday for nothing.

The woman glanced at Maddy's ID. "I've never met a necromancer before."

Maddy smiled. "We are licensed and certified by the necromancy board for the commonwealth of Massachusetts. We're just like any other medical professional, except our field is somewhat new. Which is why we have clinical trials like the one we're asking you to participate in."

The woman pointed to the end of the form. "Can you explain this section about test results are not guaranteed?"

"Yes, of course. As this is all part of clinical trials of necromantic resurrection, we use both test necromantic injections as well as control injections and can't disclose which will be used for the procedure." Maddy smiled. "Even I don't know which is which. As such, we can't guarantee full revival of the test subject."

"My Cleopatra."

Maddy resisted the urge to fidget. Client interaction was not her strong point. "Yes, your Cleopatra."

"Will she become a zombie?"

"No. There are no zombies. That's an unfortunate label given to those who have been successfully resurrected. A success means your pet will be fully revived should anything happen during this surgery to put her life at risk."

"But if it fails, is she a zombie?"

Take a deep breath. This is a teachable moment.

Maddy shook her head. "No. The vast majority of resurrections occur within moments of the cessation of respiration or heartbeat. Think of this as an additional tool your vet can use to revive your pet. A failed resurrection is no different than if a person were at the emergency room, and the doctors couldn't revive her with CPR and other tools. No partial resurrection is allowed in these clinical tests."

She knew she was edging close to falsehood, but part of the paperwork this woman was about to sign clearly stated that only a full resurrection would be allowed. Anything short of that would result in euthanasia. She considered leaving that point out of the conversation, but her conscience wouldn't let her.

Maddy put her hand on the woman's shoulder. "As this is a clinical trial, there's the chance that the resurrection won't be complete. There is no way to verify the efficacy of the necromantic test injections ahead of time. The test is used only if other traditional methods fail. Your pet, should the necromantic tests result in partial resurrection, would be allowed to pass away."

The woman nodded and continued reading the form. Maddy watched as she read past the euthanasia statement in bold at the end of the form. She held her breath until, at last, the woman scrawled her signature.

"Thank you," Maddy said as she accepted the form. "We'll do our best for Cleopatra should the need arise."

Maddy walked back and handed Andre the form. "Which room?"

"Room 103, on the left," he said.

Maddy followed his instructions and stepped into the third operating room in the facility. Two people waited for her, dressed in light-blue scrubs. The vet tech handed Maddy a mask, and she put it on, then pulled a pair of darker blue surgical gloves on.

"Thank you, Maddy," Helen said. She was the vet and Maddy's neighbor. "Cleopatra's an elderly cat, so even routine surgery poses risks. She's stable at the moment, so if you want to take a seat, we can begin."

Maddy opened her cooler and pulled out one of the two injectors she'd taken from the lab. Strictly speaking, she didn't need to keep them in a cooler with the new injector design, but old habits meant she still did. She placed the red injector on the table beside her, leaned her cane against the table, and sat on the only chair in the surgery room.

The vet tech, a young woman with two paw-print tattoos on each wrist, sat at the computer. "Can I have your license number, please?"

Maddy pulled her lanyard off and handed it to the tech, who typed in the details and gave it back to her. Maddy took out her own tablet and typed details about the cat and procedure into her database as Helen began the operation to remove a cancerous mass. Maddy watched her friend make the first incision on the cat's shaved belly.

"The tumor is more invasive than the X-ray suggested," Helen said. "This will be a tricky one."

She kept going with her procedure, but at the fifteen-minute mark, Cleopatra's vital signs began to drop. Helen glanced at the readouts but continued her efforts to remove all the cancer she could find.

At the twenty-minute mark, Cleopatra's signs flatlined.

"She needs help," Helen said. She turned to the vet tech. "Please note down the time of the necromancy injection in Cleopatra's chart." She then turned to Maddy. "You're up."

Maddy took one of the injectors and walked the few steps to the operating table.

"Will you use the IV catheter?" the vet tech asked.

Maddy held up her injector. "This is quicker." She placed the injector on the shaved patch of paw and snapped it. The blood entered the cat instantly. Maddy handed the used injector to the vet tech. "Please add the test-injector number to the cat's records and return it to me. All necromancy injectors are controlled substances and must be disposed of at registered sites." Which included Maddy's lab.

"How long do we wait?" Helen asked.

"Not long. If the test injector held necromantic blood strong enough to revive her, we'll know in seconds."

Sure enough, Cleopatra's heartbeat returned and, a moment later, her respiration.

The vet tech clapped her hands. "It worked!"

"Patience," Helen said. She glanced at Maddy. "Do we continue the procedure?"

"Wait two minutes. If it's a full resurrection, you should be safe to proceed." Two minutes took forever in Maddy's book, but it was necessary to ensure it wasn't a partial resurrection, a zombie, as the cat's owner said.

When the two-minute mark came and went, and Cleopatra's vitals remained stable, Maddy sat back in her chair while Helen finished the procedure. Maddy jotted down more notes in her tablet and waited until the operation ended before she joined Helen to give Cleopatra's owner the good news.

Helen began the conversation with the owner. "Cleopatra did extremely well, and she's resting now. We'll need to keep her overnight for observation. Her tumor was more difficult to extract than we expected." She turned to Maddy. "Thanks to Dr. Wu, we were able to revive Cleopatra, and she'll be with you for some time now that the bulk of the cancer is removed."

The owner turned to Maddy. "Thank you. Will Cleopatra be fully healed by that?"

"No. It's not a cure. It revives the body to a certain extent, but it doesn't fully cure existing conditions. The resurrected will have a shorter lifespan in general," Maddy said.

The owner nodded.

"One other thing you should be aware of," Maddy said. "In very rare circumstances, the necromancy effect is retracted. If that happens, the patient will age at an accelerated rate."

"Retracted?" the woman asked.

Maddy nodded. "Yes. We don't have good terms for this process yet in the industry, but necromancy is easiest to understand as the necromancer giving a part of their life energy to someone else. If that necromancer passes away, that life energy they shared dies with them. As this is a blind clinical trial, we can't inform you should that event occur. I can say the volunteers have all been under thirty-five years of age, so the chances of this happening are quite slim."

Maddy left Helen to describe the follow-up care and further

prognosis details. She called an Uber and waited outside for it to take her home. She'd earned herself an afternoon in bed to help ease the pain inching its way into her joints as she waited.

CHAPTER THREE

"The son and husband are still in Room 211." Tamar's boss pulled on a light jacket. "You'll want to keep a close eye. I don't expect the mother to last the night."

Tamar nodded, jotting the information in her notes.

Her boss put her hand on Tamar's shoulder. "Glad to see you looking better than you did Friday. I know it's hard, but this is why we're here, to keep the patients and family comfortable in their final days. 211 has her family here, and given the pain she's been in of late, it's a release when she finally lets go."

Tamar ducked her head. "Yes. I'll get used to it."

"No. Don't ever get used to it, hon. Your compassion makes you one of the patient favorites around here. But learning to accept and let go will help you keep going year after year." Her boss squeezed Tamar's shoulder and dropped her hand to pick up her thermos and backpack. "See you tomorrow evening."

Tamar preferred the later shifts, as that was when she could do the most good. The ward had less activity and fewer visitors. It also meant a greater risk someone would pass before family arrived, but also less risk that another nurse would see what Tamar did to resurrect some patients for a short time, in the hopes of granting them that final good-bye with loved ones.

Tamar started her rounds. Her first two patients were asleep, one naturally, the other because of the pain medications he was on. Her third patient, new to the ward, gave her a smile as she entered.

"Evening, Mrs. Zelinski. How are you feeling today?"

"Please, call me Agnes."

"Only if you call me Tamar. Did you want your bed up higher so you can watch the TV better?"

"Oh, there's nothing much on. I would like my book though."

Tamar raised the back of Agnes's bed and helped her get comfortable. She saw a pile of books on the table by the small sofa that was meant for guests and picked up the first book on the pile. "*To Kill a Mockingbird*?"

"Yes. That's the one."

Tamar glanced at the rest of the books in the pile. "A lot of classics here." She handed the book to Agnes.

Agnes smiled. "Twenty books to read before you die, that's what my late husband told me. Well, it's time I caught up, don't you think?"

Tamar returned the smile. Some patients handled their ending time with such grace. She hoped she could face her own passing with that much courage when her time came. "There's a lot in that pile I haven't read, either. Might be wise for me to read a few as well."

"You're welcome to borrow some. The second pile contains the ones I've finished."

"Might just take you up on that later."

Tamar checked her vitals and administered Agnes's medications. She wasn't on any significant ones yet, but her palliative care would increase quickly, according to her doctor's notes. "You enjoy that book. I'll be by to see you later this evening."

Tamar passed her patient Janice's teenage son in the hall outside room 211. "Off for a break?"

He nodded. "I'm getting dinner for my dad and me."

Old enough to drive, then, she thought. She was only twenty-five herself, but she wasn't good at judging age based on looks. She could tell only that the brown fuzz on his upper lip looked like it struggled to show up at all.

She had returned to the nurses' station to write her notes after her rounds when she heard the telltale beeps from Janice's monitors. Most family members wanted a medical professional around when the final moments came, just to explain what was happening, so she headed that way.

She wasn't surprised to see Janice's husband Pete in the doorway, looking frazzled. "It's okay. This is expected," she said. "Shall I come inside with you for a time?"

"It's my son. He's not back. It's my fault for mentioning I was hungry."

Tamar saw the grief and guilt on his face. The end was never easy. Well, this time, she could help. "Let me turn off the monitors for a time. Janice won't slip away that quickly," she lied. "Why don't you go out to the front lot and see if your son is back."

It was a lame excuse to get him out of the room, but it worked. Tamar turned off the monitors and closed Janice's door with a privacy curtain so no one walking by could see what she was up to.

She glanced down at the middle-aged woman. "I'm sorry to bring you back, but you made me promise your son could say his good-byes." Back when Janice still had moments of consciousness, she'd asked Tamar for that favor, not knowing to what extent Tamar could really make it happen.

With one last glance around, Tamar pulled out a needle and, with more skill than anyone should have, she jabbed her own vein and pulled out a small amount of her blood. She wished she had a better idea of how much was really needed, but she'd learned from the dozen or so times she'd done this already that little was necessary for a short-term resurrection. Sometimes the patient resurrected for a few hours, sometimes longer, but always enough.

She'd lose her nursing license if she were found out, but no one was around to see her pull the needle off the syringe and empty exactly one milliliter of her blood into Janice's mouth. Tamar felt the familiar tug inside her. She couldn't explain it if she tried, but she knew a part of her was being transferred into Janice. She couldn't see anything visually, but it felt like a cord of light spread from her to the woman in the bed. She stuffed the used medical device inside a surgical glove as Janice's eyes fluttered and her breath returned to a steady cadence.

She flicked on the monitors as Pete and his son rushed back into the room. The boy looked far younger than he had moments ago, but grief had a way of doing that, especially to teens, she'd learned. "It's okay. She's stabilized. I turned the monitors back on for now. I'll leave you three alone."

Tamar spent the rest of her shift with the usual fatigue that came from resurrecting a person, even for a short time. Janice would last the night, but not much longer. Her family stayed with her throughout.

❖

Tamar stepped into her old, used blue Prius, tried to rub the sleep out of her eyes, and started her commute back home. She wanted to go straight there but needed food for Kalev, and that meant a visit to the specialty pet store in Beverly. Traffic hadn't quite picked up yet for the morning commute, so it was a fast ride on the highway to the next town over.

Less than a half mile in front of her, Tamar watched in horror as a small yellow mini swerved to avoid something in the roadway, smashed into the railing on the right, and flipped. Tamar's nursing instincts took over, and she pulled over behind the disabled car, leaving her emergency lights flashing.

She dialed 911. "There's been a car accident." She gave their location and informed the dispatcher that she was a nurse.

Tamar tossed her phone onto the seat of her car and raced

to the upended vehicle. She crouched down, reached into the broken driver window, and checked for vitals.

"Shoot." The middle-aged male driver had no pulse. He wasn't in a position where she could start CPR, and she didn't think she'd have the strength to pull him out of the wreckage.

She also didn't have her equipment with her to cleanly draw her own blood and give it to him. "Shoot, shoot, shoot." She rocked back on her heels. Time meant everything, and time wasn't on this man's side. She listened for the sound of approaching emergency help, but nothing came other than the occasional car passing by.

"On your own with this one," she said to herself. She looked around at her options. Car safety glass wouldn't help, but a broken glass bottle lay shattered by the roadside. "I'm going to regret this," she mumbled as she grabbed it, pulled a disinfecting swap from her scrubs, and wiped it as clean as she could.

With a deep grunt, she sliced her palm. "Son of a beach wagon!" That hurt.

Her blood oozed out from the stinging cut. She caught sight of flashing lights in the distance but didn't stop. The man's life was on the line. He hung from his seat belt in the upended car. She reached her bloody hand in and smeared her palm across his open mouth, squeezing her blood inside it.

She knew the moment her necromancy kicked in when a wave of exhaustion knocked her on her backside. This time, what was usually the sensation of a cord of light between her and the patient turned into a river of energy flowing out from her to him. Her eyes drifted shut as the flashing lights approached and pulled up behind her car.

"Not an ambulance," she muttered, glad she'd used her blood to revive the man. She must have blacked out because suddenly an Asian man in a black suit was squatting down next to her.

"Are you licensed?" he asked.

Tamar pulled out her wallet with her uninjured hand and passed it to him with her license picture showing.

"No, not driver's license. Necromancy license."

Tamar wasn't following his logic as her eyes drifted shut again. The next moment she heard him talking on the phone.

"I need you to look up Tamar Richler."

Tamar forced her eyelids open. "I'm right here."

The man shook his head, but he winked and smiled, a kind smile. He nodded to whatever the person on the phone said to him.

He looked up at the sound of sirens. "No. I'm fine. A resurrection."

"Meet me at Beverly Hospital, say in two hours," he said. "No. I'm not drained. I'll explain later." He hung up and put a hand on Tamar's shoulder. "It's okay. You'll be okay. You overdid it."

Tamar's eyes drifted shut again until she felt a sting in her arm.

"It's fine," he said, pulling his first vial of blood from her arm. "This is just for verification."

Tamar didn't know what had to be verified. She didn't much care because exhaustion drained her to the point she passed out.

❖

Maddy hung up the phone and dropped back down onto her bed. She tried to return to sleep, but that effort failed. Her sluggish mind churned on Kenneth's enigmatic call about a woman named Tamar and his insistence that Maddy meet him at the hospital. After a futile ten minutes, she gave up hope of more sleep and sat up.

Every major joint from her wrists to her ankles hurt. She didn't need a weather app to know a storm front was approaching. She glanced at the spare cane by the bed and ignored it. She wouldn't resort to it in her own apartment. Instead, she used the furniture to help guide her to the bathroom, where she pulled out two ankle braces. Too agitated for a soak in the tub, she took a quick, hot shower, dried, and sat on the edge of the tub to strap on each ankle brace. It did nothing for the pain but helped her stability.

Dressed in black slacks and a rose blouse, she was ready to go in less than an hour. She could wait it out, or she could call an Uber and hunt Kenneth down at the hospital and get some answers. Hunting him was the easy choice. The next choice was less easy. She paced her apartment, from living room to kitchen and back, then sighed and grabbed her good cane by the apartment front door. Today was a double-protection kind of day to be sure an ankle wouldn't simply give out on her.

Time to see what Kenneth was up to now.

Maddy arrived at the hospital forty-five minutes early and stepped into the already-busy ER. She walked to the admin desk. "I'm looking for Kenneth Wu," she said.

The woman checked her computer. "I'm sorry. That name isn't listed here."

Maddy tried to rack her foggy brain for the name he'd given her, but it wouldn't come back. "Thanks," she said and stepped away. She sat in the waiting room and called him.

"Where are you?" she asked.

"You're early, but we're in the ER. Tell them you're with Tamar Richler."

That's the name! She went to the locked ER door and buzzed in as a visitor for Tamar. The nursing station let her in and directed her to one of the curtained rooms off to the left. The ER had more than its fair share of beds, including a few lined up around the edges of the nursing station.

Kenneth waited for her outside one of the curtained beds.

"You need to pace your resurrections better," she said, though she didn't see the telltale signs of exhaustion around his eyes.

He glanced around and pulled her to the side, away from the bustling nurses and orderlies. "This is an interesting case, but you need to keep silent on what I'm about to tell you."

Maddy frowned but nodded.

He pointed back to the bed where presumably the Tamar woman was. "She was first on the scene at a car accident. Maddy, she did a full resurrection." He held up his hand. "Based on a cut on her own palm."

He sounded elated. She had a different opinion. "Reckless."

He waved a hand. "Possibly. She's not licensed. I arrived at the scene before the ambulance so took responsibility for the resurrection."

"Kenneth! You risk your license for that."

"And she risked prison to keep someone alive. This is why we're fighting for the Good Samaritan Act, Maddy. To keep people like her safe."

She crossed her arms. "People like her should be registered. And if she'd taken training like she should have, she'd be licensed and not in legal trouble. Shit, Kenneth. Why are you doing this for some stranger?"

He smiled. "There was a time when we were reckless, too, to save our brother."

That wasn't fighting fair. She sighed and dropped her arms. "That didn't go well for our brother Aiden or us, did it? I'm disabled. Aiden is at home in a permanent coma, and look at you. Your hair is already going gray from the strain."

He stepped back, definitely self-conscious about his visible aging.

"Sorry," Maddy said. "I'm just tired."

He nodded, his bright smile returning. "Tropical storm's coming up the coast. That always gives you trouble. Come on. I'd like you to meet her."

She followed him into the curtained area where a woman who looked remarkably young lay on a gurney, her eyes closed. She appeared peaceful, with her halo of black, curly hair surrounding an elfin face. "She looks in her teens. How old is she?"

Kenneth made a little loose-and-free with the woman's wallet to pull out her driver's license. "She's twenty-five."

Definitely not as young as she looked. Maddy stepped closer and nearly jumped when a warm hand covered hers where she held onto the gurney's safety bar. Deep-brown eyes stared back up at her.

"Hey, gorgeous," Tamar said.

Maddy withdrew her hand and glared at Kenneth.

He held up a hand. "She's exhausted. Probably doesn't even know what she's saying."

"Are you my doctor?" Tamar asked.

Maddy looked back at her. "No. I'm a researcher."

"Oh. Why are you here? And where is here?"

"Here is the Beverly Hospital, and you're in the ER. As for why I'm here, I'm not sure myself," Maddy said, glaring at her brother.

Kenneth stepped into Tamar's view. "I introduced myself before, but I'm Kenneth Wu, Necromancer Marshal for the Commonwealth of Massachusetts. You're here because of an accident." He held up a hand before Tamar could respond. "We can talk details later, but for now, I recommend you rest. We'll move you to another location in a few hours."

Tamar's eyes drifted shut again on that comment. She really was a pretty woman, if reckless with her skills. Maddy looked back at her brother. "We need to talk."

"Yes, we do. Let's grab breakfast."

❖

Breakfast came in the form of coffee and a croissant from the hospital café, but it was a noisy enough environment that Maddy felt safe grilling Kenneth.

"First off, you're risking your career, and I still don't understand why," she said.

"You don't buy the Good Samaritan defense from me?" he said with the boyish grin she remembered from their childhood and just frowned in return.

"Okay. You got me there. She's not just a young woman in need of help, and she's not just a pretty face, though I know you think so, too. She's definitely your type."

Maddy rolled her eyes. "I'm not interested in dating your rescue patient, Kenneth."

He laughed. "Maybe you should be. When was the last time you went out on a date?"

"When was the last time you did?" she fired back.

"Yeah. We're not exactly making waves in that area, are we? Even Dad's getting on my case about that now. Text messages from France on my love life. Did you know they're selling their condo and moving to Marseilles for the warmer weather?"

Maddy put down her croissant. "You're deflecting the conversation to our globe-trotting parents. Answer the question. Why are you interested in Tamar Richler?"

"You always are straight to the point, Maddy. Okay. I'll reiterate what I told you earlier. She fully resurrected an accident fatality. With blood. From her hand. After she'd done, I guess, the same thing at work."

"And?"

"You must be tired," he said. "This is a double resurrection by any measure. With unrestricted transference of necromantic power. Can you imagine what she might be capable of with actual training?"

Maddy leaned forward. "And can you imagine the damage she might have done to herself?" She tapped her cane that hung from the side of the table. "This could be her future, already."

Kenneth sipped his coffee before answering. "This is why I want your help. She needs training, but also someone to explore what she can do, and where, if any, she's already injured herself. You must admit, you're uniquely qualified to help her."

Maddy sat back in her chair. He had valid points, but then he always had valid points. "I liked it better when you were a kid and left all the logic and manipulation to Aiden."

Something passed in Kenneth's eyes. "I like to think I learned from my twin. I was too soft, too unrealistic back then."

While she missed the old carefree and compassionate Kenneth of their childhood, she regretted her flash of anger. They'd both suffered when the accident happened that had left Aiden in a coma for the past fourteen years.

"What are you proposing?" she asked.

"Come home. The house is big enough for you and Tamar to stay while she recuperates. I have my condo in Boston, so you won't have me looking over your shoulder. And you can start lessons right away. With her condition, I can get her on short-term disability leave from her job. She'll need that anyway."

Maddy hoped for Tamar's sake it stayed short-term, but she kept that to herself. "I don't much like the idea of living with a complete stranger."

"Our parents left us a huge house. We could set up another room like Aiden's on the same floor, complete with hospital bed and monitors, if she needs it. Luis can help out."

"Luis is Aiden's nurse and caregiver. He's busy enough."

Kenneth gave her a sad smile. "Aiden doesn't require much, hour to hour. I think Luis could handle another patient for a few weeks."

He was probably right, but she still hated the notion of a stranger so near her brother. It made sense, though, to keep Tamar and Aiden in close proximity while they were at the house. Her own bedroom was the farthest room from Aiden's, on the second floor, but that meant stairs every day.

"Okay. We'll try it. But I still need access to my lab. I won't give up my research for this pet project of yours."

"Done. Expense the Uber drives to my office." He reached across the table to hold her hand. "This will be worth it for both of us. You'll see."

"Ever the optimist," she said with a smirk.

After breakfast, Maddy stepped outside the hospital to wait

for her Uber. She had a lot to prepare for with the new task ahead of her. While it would be great to be at their family home for a time and to see Aiden, it meant handing off a series of experiments to her lab assistants and packing for an extended stay.

Before then, though, she had an appointment at the statehouse to keep this afternoon. She sat outside the hospital on a low cement wall surrounding a garden with the burnt-orange and yellow hardy mums that were ubiquitous in New England this time of year. Eyes shut, she basked in the still-warm September sunlight, a moment of respite until the beep on her phone said her ride was here.

Time to get going with the day.

CHAPTER FOUR

Tamar felt like her eyes had been glued shut. She fought against her exhaustion to open them and look around. She was still in the same hospital bed she remembered seeing during one of her awake times. This time, though, she was alone but could hear the high level of activity happening beyond the drab blue curtain that separated her from the rest of the emergency room. A black TV screen hung on the wall in front of her, while her fake-wood side table had not so much as a cup of water on it.

She shut her eyes and felt herself start to drift off again. "No. No more sleeping."

She pulled herself more upright, but her movement jostled the IV in her arm, and something started frantically beeping. She tried to readjust herself, but nothing seemed to turn off that incessant beep. A nurse bustled in a few minutes later.

"You're awake now," he said. "How are you feeling?"

"Like I could sleep for a month."

He fiddled with her IV and monitor, and the beeping stopped. "I bet. Mr. Wu said he had to give you a significant sedative at the accident scene. It's no wonder it's taken you a few hours to recover."

Tamar frowned. "Accident?"

He pulled up her wrist to put a pulse-and-oxygen monitor on her finger. "Yes, the car accident this morning? You were first on scene." He gave her a look straight out of Compassionate 101. "That must have been traumatic for you to witness. Luckily the necromancer marshal was there to revive the victim. All's well that ends well, eh?"

Necromancer marshal? The details were fuzzy, but Tamar remembered enough to know she was in deep trouble. "Can I leave now?"

She tried to sit up, but the effort left her winded. The nurse jotted down her readings on a little notepad. "Best you stay here a bit longer, until the doctor comes around. Your pulse is elevated. You might need to stay overnight for observation."

Tamar had never spent a night in a hospital. She'd had her fair share of sprains as a kid, but nothing serious. She took a deep breath. "I would rather go home. Nothing's wrong with me, right?" Nothing except feeling exhausted and oddly cold.

Another man pulled back the curtain. "No. Nothing that a good bit of rest won't take care of." His face was familiar, but Tamar couldn't pinpoint why. He was dressed in a sharp suit, his black hair short around the ears but longer on top, like he was trying to hold on to a youth belied by the graying at his temples and wrinkles on his face. The neatly trimmed beard and mustache were reminiscent of someone again trying to present as younger than he was. Nanna had taught her how to read people, and what Tamar read here was someone not willing to accept he was inching into his forties.

He held out a hand. "Good afternoon, Tamar. Do you remember me?"

She lifted her hand, and he did all the work of shaking and letting go. "Sort of?"

He turned back to the nurse. "Can you get the floor doctor, please? I'd like to discuss Tamar's release."

When the nurse left, the man pulled the plastic visitor chair closer to her bed and sat. "I'm Kenneth Wu, and we have quite a bit to talk about before the doctor comes. Luckily ER doctors are busy people, so we have some time."

This is it, she thought. I'm in trouble now. The adrenaline pumping into her system now fought off some of the extreme fatigue, and she sat up straighter.

"First off," he said, "you aren't on a sedative. That was just a convenient excuse for your exhaustion. What you're feeling now is clinically called transient necromantic fatigue, brought on in your case from extended necromantic transference. From what you were saying at the accident scene, this was your second resurrection attempt in a single day, correct?"

She could deny it, but what would lying do for her right now? She just nodded.

"Well, I can't tell you how dangerous that is, but I'm sure my sister will go into it in detail later."

The vision of a beautiful woman with long, black hair with brown highlights flashed in Tamar's memory, as did a sinking feeling she'd said something stupid. Not a surprise, really. Tamar tended to become awkward around women she was attracted to.

"You need to understand a couple of important points, Tamar. While what you did was courageous, and you saved a life, it is still considered illegal in this state to conduct a resurrection without a license."

She winced. "How much trouble am I in, sir?"

He smiled with a wink. "Kenneth, please. You are in fact incredibly lucky on many accounts. A double resurrection could have put you in a coma. That it didn't shows the extent of your potential as a resurrector, and for that you should feel proud."

"I don't feel proud. I feel I'm in deep trouble, and you're cushioning the blow for me."

"Well, let me get to the second account on which you're lucky. I received the 911 contact and was first on the scene. Besides you, me, and my sister, no one knows the resurrection was yours. Now, I'm not one to regularly steal credit, but in this instance, it was better if I claimed the resurrection in your stead."

Tamar studied his expression and frowned. "That's kind of you." And not realistic in her mind, not for the necromancer marshal. Something was in it for him, but she felt too foggy to ask.

"The last item where you're lucky," he said, "is that my sister is updating the necromancy curriculum and certification."

"I'm sorry," she said. "I'm not making the connection on that one."

"Well, in return for keeping our little secret, I'll require that you get licensed. As you can see, an unlicensed necromancer can be dangerous to herself and others."

And that's the catch, she thought. No gift comes free. "I work full-time. When are the classes?"

He held up a hand. "Let me take one small step back to explain what transient necromantic fatigue is. That feeling of exhaustion you have right now? That's going to get worse, not better, over the next couple of weeks. After that, with rest, and limiting your necromantic exposure, you may recover fully. On the other hand, you may not."

"Shoot. Will I have this for the rest of my life, then?"

His expression turned sympathetic. "We hope that won't be the case, but given the unique circumstances here, I can't recommend anyone more experienced at handling this than my sister, Maddy."

All in the family, she thought. Still, time with a beautiful woman could have its perks, even if only in her head. She scooted up in the bed again to try energizing her tired brain. "Can you lay out exactly what you're saying here?"

"To the point. I like that. So the point is—you have a recovery period of at least a couple of months. You won't be able to return to your job during that time. I have an associate who can sign off on short-term disability to cover that situation for you. Meanwhile, you need special care and shouldn't be home alone."

Tamar shut her eyes to block the tears about to come. "I guess I can call my grandmother in Western Massachusetts." Returning wouldn't be the worst thing. Facing her grandmother with the reason for it—overextending her untrained necromantic talent—now that would be painful.

"I have an alternate idea in mind. Maddy has agreed to take on your training as a personal tutor."

Now that got Tamar's pulse rising.

"But of course, she's not going out to Western Massachusetts. I have a place right here in Beverly where you could stay, and Maddy could teach you."

Tamar was too tired to think things through. "Okay, but I have a dog as well."

"That's fine, so long as he gets along with a tortoise."

Tortoise? Tamar didn't ask. "This all seems…"

"Too good to be true?" he asked.

Convenient, she thought, but she didn't air her doubts. She was in enough legal trouble. If she just followed through on this plan of his, she'd get out without a felony and, from the sound of it, with a necromancy license, like she'd always wanted. So why was she resisting?

"I know this is a lot to throw at you all at once. Let's start with the basics. You need help once you're discharged. Let me send an assistant to help you pack some clothes and get your dog, and you can stay at my place for a couple of weeks. If it doesn't work out, we can find alternate accommodations."

That sounded reasonable. "Okay."

He left a few minutes later to make the arrangements. Tamar knew enough about ERs to know she'd be here for another few hours anyway. She grabbed her phone from her pocket and texted her cousin.

Can you swing by and take Kalev out for me, please? I'm in the ER.

Samantha's call came in fast. "Are you okay?"

"Yes. Just brought in after an accident. Not me, someone else." Tamar went with Kenneth's lie for now. "I guess I fainted."

"The nurse fainted. Must have been some accident."

"I'll explain later, please." Tamar couldn't mask the yawn. "I doubt they'll let me out of here for a bit."

"Okay. I'll go spoil your dog. But I want to hear all about this when you get out."

"Happy to," she said. Assuming she'd know what all this was about for real by then.

She should be thinking this over more carefully. She should be planning, but all she could do was lean back and let the fatigue take control for now. Time enough to panic later.

❖

Maddy walked into the golden-domed Massachusetts Statehouse and prepared herself for the battle to come. The long walk up the stone steps to the second story did not improve her mood. She glanced into the empty House chambers, with wood-paneled walls and paintings of historic moments in Massachusetts history, but she would not testify in front of the full legislature today. No. She had one special session with the judiciary committee, with one special woman who seemed out to get Kenneth, and her, by extension, for being his sister.

And that special woman met her at the doors to the committee room.

"Good morning, Ms. Wu."

"Mrs. Bunte." If Jasmine Bunte refused to call her Dr. Wu, she could play that same card and not refer to her as Representative Bunte of Brockton.

Jasmine wore her usual gray skirt suit with a black-and-white-checkered scarf around her neck. She'd trimmed her graying hair since the last time Maddy had to sit opposite her. The straightened bob that surrounded Jasmine's brown face made it appear as if she were trying to recapture her youth, but Maddy knew better. Jasmine Bunte might seem a healthy, vibrant fifty-five, but she was a fading thirty-five—premature aging that came hand in glove with the resurrected.

Jasmine opened the wood-paneled door and waved Maddy to precede her. Maddy gripped her cane and walked past her. Kenneth would give her grief for not leaving the cane at home, but he didn't have to worry about falling on his face in front of the entire judiciary committee.

Jasmine stepped in beside her as if they were old friends. "I convinced the committee to let you answer questions from the front-row table instead of the podium."

Maddy raised her eyebrows. "That's considerate of you."

Jasmine put a hand on her elbow. "We may be on opposite sides of this issue, Dr. Wu, but we share a common ground in our current health situation. Insisting on anyone standing through this meeting is ablest nonsense."

Maddy gave her a tight smile and proceeded to her seat, not sure how to take that olive branch from her political opponent, especially when she knew Jasmine hated her brother, Kenneth. She glanced around the small chamber with its white walls and modern row of tables and seats in an arc before the raised committee bench. Three committee members already sat in their high chairs: two men in suits and ties, and another woman wearing a black pantsuit and red blouse. Maddy adjusted the collar of her rose blouse and waited for the proceedings to begin.

With all the pomp that made politics a drawn-out episode, the committee began its work. The main topic for the day was HR 5239.

The committee chairman invited Maddy to give her testimony. Thankful for the ability to do so seated, Maddy leaned into the microphone. "Honorable committee members, while I respect the passions ignited by the legalization of necromancy in this state and across the country, this divisive issue need not impact the existing laws. The Good Samaritan law was passed years ago to protect those who volunteer to help others in good faith. The existing law equally protects the professional and the layperson from liabilities that may present from an act of kindness in an emergency situation."

"If I may," Jasmine said, "your conflation of professional and amateur leaves out some critical factors. Doctors should not have to face litigation if they provide emergency medical care at a restaurant. We can all agree on that. But we also can agree that my fifteen-year-old nephew shouldn't attempt a tracheostomy on his choking classmate because he saw it on a YouTube video."

"I fail to see your point, Representative." Maddy's tension began to rise.

"Let me clarify for you, dear. On the one hand, you want professional status for your necromancers. Or at least your brother, the necromancer marshal does. Correct?"

"Yes."

"And this is clearly covered under the existing law." Jasmine turned to her fellow committee members. "It should equally be clear that we cannot extend that legal protection to all necromancy attempts, licensed or unlicensed. We have to have checks and balances against this type of situation."

"Respectfully, Representative, an unlicensed necromancer is not equivalent to your nephew and his YouTube videos. An unlicensed necromancer, especially an underage necromancer, may not even be aware of their abilities until a necromantic event is triggered. Your nephew with his knife at the throat of the choking victim could just as easily nick the finger of his sister who tried to stop him. And were she a necromancer, her blood could impact that victim without her even being aware that it's possible."

"Yes. Yes, Dr. Wu. A valid point, and one we should be addressing with mandatory necromancer registration, but that is not before the committee today."

Mandatory registration? Did Kenneth know this was something else up Jasmine's sleeve? A knot grew in Maddy's stomach.

"Yes. To the point at hand," Maddy said. "We don't prosecute people who pull someone out of a burning car, whether that event triggered more injuries or not. Such people did the best they could to help someone. Similarly, necromancers, licensed or unlicensed, are doing the best they are able to save a life."

"A life the victim has no choice in determining," Jasmine said. "A life that can never be the life God intended it to be."

Oh, now she's pulling the God card? Two could play at that. "That same God gave the rescuers their necromancy abilities. We don't judge the EMT or bystander doing emergency CPR, regardless of the outcome."

"Perhaps we should," Jasmine said. "But again, not the focus of today's meeting and the proposed bill in front of us now. As my esteemed colleagues know, resurrection comes with a cost, a cost most of us are unaware of and have no say in when the resurrection occurs. I don't wish to complicate this meeting, but I am the poster child for what can go wrong, am I not?"

She most certainly was not, but Maddy kept her mouth shut. It wouldn't help her case at all to bring up her brother Aiden's fourteen-year-long coma after her own botched resurrection attempt. Hell. Maybe Jasmine had a point that Maddy just didn't want to hear. Maybe she should be accountable for the state she left her own brother in.

"As our esteemed guest recalls, my life was returned to me by her own brother, right after he received his license. Now I am grateful for his efforts."

The hell she was, Maddy thought. Jasmine blamed Kenneth for everything that went wrong in her life after that resurrection.

"And yet, the impact on my life is obvious. I have arthritis in both hips, and my lung capacity weakens every year. My life expectancy went from eighty to sixty, if I am lucky."

Maddy felt the mood of the meeting change and had to do something. "That is another area we are researching. We still don't know so much about necromancy, but our ability to help those resurrected to live full lives is one of my main focuses."

"Yes, and we thank you for that, Dr. Wu," Jasmine said. "But the fact remains, today, we, as you say, do not know as much as we should. Doesn't that suggest we proceed with caution and strong guardrails?"

The rest of the meeting continued in the same vein, with different committee members asking questions that pontificated their views more than asking anything they really wanted Maddy to answer, but she kept going, pressing her point to protect necromancers from falling under the restrictions proposed by a prejudiced view against them.

❖

Maddy rested on her cane as she faced the long, white, stone staircase down to the first level. Christ on a cracker, she didn't want to deal with this staircase right now. Her ankles were swollen from sitting so long in one position during the committee hearing, and the ache traveled up her calves to her knees. Members of Congress, local lobbyists, and statehouse visitors rushed past her on their way to lunch.

A hand on her elbow paused Maddy's effort to proceed down the stairs.

"Dr. Wu," Jasmine said. "Please, come with me to the congressional elevator. These stairs are just a bear to deal with after a long meeting."

Maddy hesitated.

Jasmine pointed the way. "There's no need for us to be antagonists outside that committee room. We both hold strong opinions—you for your necromancers, me for my constituents. But we have one thing in common."

"Which is?" Maddy asked.

"A hatred for these stairs! My hip is acting up, and I'm guessing you're not too keen on trudging down them as well. We can help each other, you know. And today, I can help you with an alternative not open to the public. Come on. I'll tell you more about my nephew and niece. Seems only fair if you'll be using them to make a point in our hearing sessions, right?"

Maddy smiled and followed Jasmine back down the corridor. "Thanks for the assistance."

"No problem, Doctor. I'm sure you'll have an opportunity in the future to return the favor."

That remark would have sounded innocent from anyone else, but Jasmine Bunte had a way of making her feel like a child, even if their chronological ages were separated by only five years.

It wasn't until the elevator doors closed that Maddy noticed the pin on Jasmine's lapel—a stylized zombie head with the words "Zombie rights are Human rights" written in a circle around the head.

She pointed to it. "That term doesn't offend you?"

Jasmine glanced down at her pin and laughed. "My father was a military man. He taught me when I was a child that the best way to defeat an enemy is to destroy their ammunition. The bigots in this world are against both of us. I'm sure they have choice words for you as well."

"That they do." Maddy could think of a few she'd been called, including witch, satanist, and the devil.

"Even members of my own family think I have no soul," Jasmine said.

"That's horrible."

"Prejudice knows no bounds, Dr. Wu, as you well realize. People call my kind zombies and think it's both clever and painful. But that just made us more determined to take that slur and make it our own. So yes, I'm a zombie, and I'm proud of it. And this little pin comes from the Zombie Advocacy Group. You'd be surprised how many people look at it and start to shift their views on us all."

The elevator doors opened on the first floor of the statehouse. "The public exit is over to your left, down the corridor, and then take a right at the next corridor. It's been a pleasure, Dr. Wu. I'm sure we'll get a chance to chat again soon."

Jasmine walked off to the right, and Maddy headed to the left with more to think about than she'd planned after that long meeting. More than her exhausted brain wanted to consider about a woman she'd assumed was her enemy, and probably still was, on most issues.

CHAPTER FIVE

Tamar sat on her own bed, wearing her thickest sweater and wishing she could just lie back and go to sleep. Kenneth was right about the extreme fatigue not leaving anytime soon. It had been hours since she did the full resurrection, and she could still barely keep her eyelids open. Good thing Kenneth had sent along his reluctant assistant, Jen Dulek, to play chauffeur for Tamar for the day. No way would Tamar be safe to drive in this condition, and drive they would.

"Our next stop is Peterborough," Tamar said, glancing up at the young woman leaning against her bedroom doorway, staring at her phone.

Jen's dark eyebrows pulled down into the deepest frown Tamar had seen in ages. "I agreed to help you pack and take you to my boss's home."

Jen's tone indicated just what she thought of that unusual situation. Did Jen have a thing for Kenneth and see Tamar as a rival? If she weren't so tired, she'd laugh at that one. Tamar liked women, though this one was definitely not her type. "Helping me pack includes helping me get my dog to my grandmother's. I don't know how long I'll be at Kenneth's place." It was a stretch, but as she packed, she realized the wide-open spaces of her grandmother's farm in western Massachusetts would be a better place for her dog than someone else's house. Maybe it was paranoia, but Tamar was stepping into the unknown, and she'd feel better knowing her dog was well taken care of.

"Fine. Are we done here?"

"Just one last thing." Tamar texted her grandmother to prepare her for their arrival. She knew she'd have some serious explanations to give once she arrived, but with an annoyed Jen at her side, Tamar would escape more quickly than if she'd been alone. With the open-ended *I'll explain when I get there* text sent, Tamar clipped on Kalev's lead, and he tugged her out the apartment door, ready for whatever adventure lay ahead. Tamar wished she shared his enthusiasm.

The two-hour drive to Peterborough went by quickly since Tamar slept through most of it. Kalev sat quietly in his car harness in the back seat of Jen's black SUV, but that didn't keep Jen from glaring at him through her rearview mirror when they left Tamar's apartment. Jen had that same scowl and glare when Tamar woke up from the slower movement of the car.

They entered the center of Peterborough in a minor slowdown of evening traffic. Nestled between the Deerfield River and the rolling Berkshire hills, the town sported the usual white Congregational church that most New England towns had. The red-brick and white-trimmed old Presbyterian church dominated the main intersection, though. No longer a place of worship, it housed the town's main claim to fame—a series of boutique shops where local artisans sold anything from handmade sweaters, to pottery, to dried herbs and specialty soaps.

They passed through the town, and Tamar took over the directions since map apps never quite got the instructions correct, even after years.

She directed Jen down two side streets and up one long, winding road into the hillside that formed the outer edge of Peterborough. Some trees showed their early fall colors, but most maintained their summer green.

"Take the left ahead."

Jen slowed down, setting her blinker for the nonexistent traffic around them. "That one?" She pointed.

"That one. Yes." Tamar hid her smile at Jen's horror of having to drive her sparkling SUV down a dirt road as if they were leaving all civilization behind.

The sensation of moving from pavement to dirt and gravel perked up her sleeping dog, and Kalev sat up and wagged his tail. This time, Tamar felt a bit of his enthusiasm. She'd lived here with her grandmother for ten years after her mom died, and she loved the sense of peace it meant to her. The dirt road started the border of her grandmother's farm property as it wound its way through oak and pine until it opened to a set of rolling pastures with midsized gray, white, and black Shetland sheep munching away in the fading sunlight.

Jen pulled up in front of the red-painted barn adjacent to the main house, and Tamar let Kalev out. He ran straight for the house, where Tamar's grandmother stepped out.

"Hello, Kalev, you beastie!" Her grandmother gave him a scratch and a treat from her pocket, and he bounded off to investigate the property. Her grandmother, dressed in a green sweater and matching scarf, turned back to the two human visitors. "Welcome," she said, holding out a hand. "And thank you for driving my granddaughter this far out. Come inside. I have lemonade waiting."

To Tamar's surprise, Jen didn't pinch her brow at the thought of some old woman's homemade lemonade but stepped inside with enthusiasm.

Tamar's enthusiasm started to fade as she considered just how to explain all this to her grandmother.

❖

"So you're telling me, Tamar, that you not only did something reckless, but now you plan to spend the next month or two recuperating in the home of the necromancer marshal?"

Tamar swallowed a mouthful of cool lemonade. She saw Jen's smirk out of the corner of her eye. Kenneth had made it clear he trusted his assistant, so no need to hide who'd done the resurrection. Still, there was no polite way to tell Jen to wait in the car while Tamar explained things. So, they all sat like best friends on her grandmother's back porch in wicker chairs as the splash of glowing orange clouds faded to gray with the setting sun.

"It was an accident, Nanna. What was I supposed to do? Ignore it?"

"Wait for the ambulance, child."

"There's no way to know if the ambulance would have had a necromancer on staff. We aren't that common."

"It's 'we' already? Tamar, you know how I feel about this. Necromancy might be legal now, but it's barely tolerated. The tide can and will turn, as it always does to those who aren't part of the majority culture. Pogroms aren't just our Jewish past. The equivalent happens in every culture and has already happened to necromancers in other places."

It was a familiar argument. Her grandmother's decades as a Jewish philosopher meant Tamar would never win this one. "I know, Nanna. But hiding won't change who I am."

"I thought you were happy as a nurse, but now you want to become a licensed necromancer."

Wanted? Yes. Had to now in order to hide her crime? Also yes. "I don't have to practice, but I do need the legal coverage of a license."

Her grandmother leaned back in her chair, her brown eyes on the darkened silhouette of her apple orchard in front of them. "You and I know that's not what will happen." She sighed and rested her lemonade glass on the arm of her chair. "I suppose I should have let you get training when you were a teen."

"You homeschooled me. I understand why you did it, and I'm glad you did." Tamar didn't want her grandmother to feel guilty about her choices. "I know you kept me from Mom at the end for good reasons, and you were right." She held her grandmother's hand, surprised at how thin and small it felt in her own. "This morning's accident is proof enough. If I'd been there when Mom passed, I would have tried to bring her back."

"I know, Tamar. I know. The two of you were two peas in a pod after your father left, and you were too young to fully understand the pain your mother was in from the cancer."

Tamar knew. She'd seen it. But her grandmother was right. "I'd have brought her back because I wasn't ready to let her go."

Her grandmother squeezed her hand. "Rabbi Moshe Feinstein taught us well what was to come with medical interventions on those nearing death."

Tamar smiled. "I remember your lessons on avoiding excess suffering. And he's right, even if he didn't know about necromancy at the time."

Her grandmother laughed. "Oh, he knew. It may not have been legal in his time, but like everything else in human culture, if the ability is there, someone will be using it. For good, or for ill, resurrections happened behind closed doors for centuries."

Her grandmother stood up. "Enough of an old woman's worries. You have someplace to be, and I'm sure your friend Jen would like to get on with it so she can reach her own home."

They walked back into the kitchen. "Jen, dear, would you go into the barn for me, please? You'll see boxes of apples just to the right as you enter. Take a box, for you and for your boss, as a small token of my appreciation for what you're doing to help my granddaughter."

To Tamar's surprise, Jen complied without so much as a smirk. Her grandmother had ways to make others feel at ease that Tamar wished she'd inherited.

As soon as Jen was out of earshot, her grandmother clutched Tamar's wrist. "You venture into the unknown now. Remember who you are and what you stand for. But mostly, remember you can come here at any point, should you need to."

Tamar hugged her grandmother, feeling again more bone than muscle. "I will, as soon as this is over." She pulled back. "I think this is what I need right now, this training. I know you'll worry, but I promise, I'll be fine."

Once again, Tamar spent most of the drive back to Beverly in a dead sleep. This time, she didn't notice the changing car speed and, to her embarrassment, woke up with Jen shaking her shoulder. She wiped her tired eyes and stepped out of the car to look up at what any sane person would call a mansion. The gravel drive led past perfectly manicured lawns bordered by sculpted shrubs until it ended at a four-stall garage. Jen parked in front of the white garage door closest to the yellow clapboard house that easily had ten bedrooms scattered throughout its sprawling two-floor footprint.

Jen led the way, pulling both of Tamar's suitcases behind her. Tamar followed with her backpack on her shoulders as they entered the house. The foyer opened up two stories, with white-panel half walls, the top half painted light yellow. Jen headed up the carpeted staircase. Tamar followed, then glanced back down the stairs but couldn't see much more of the first floor other than the wooden arched doorways that led into other rooms. The staircase ended up being the only carpet so far, ending at the light-wood floor, actual wood, not laminate, that stretched down the hallway.

Jen turned into the last bedroom on the right and dropped Tamar's luggage at the edge of an old wooden chest of drawers that looked like an expensive antique. "This is your room. Enjoy your stay."

Tamar resisted the urge to offer Jen a tip. She figured alienating Kenneth's assistant even more was probably not a good idea. She took in her new room, with its full-sized poster bed and light-peach walls, hoping she'd made the right decision. Either way, she didn't have it in her to do much more than pull back the rose-colored duvet and crawl into bed. She knew she really should get up and close the bedroom door, but sleep took over instead.

❖

Maddy sat in the dark sunroom of her family home with the lights off so she could see the moon riding high above the ocean waves in the distance. With her feet up on a yellow hassock, she could almost drift off to sleep, but her racing thoughts wouldn't let go that easily. She sipped a concoction of lemon balm and chamomile tea, a special brew Aiden's nurse, Louis, made for her whenever she visited. The herbal blend melted away her worries over time as the gibbous moon slipped out of view, leaving only its reflection behind on the rolling waves of the Atlantic.

Someone came in, their voices distant and indistinct. Her moment of peace shattered, she finished her tea, picked up her cane, and headed into the house. The voices had moved to the upstairs, but at this point she could tell one of them was Kenneth's assistant, Jen. Maddy made an effort to ignore Jen's pinched expression as she stomped back down the front staircase.

"Good evening, Jen," she said.

"Hardly." Jen paused at the last step, glaring back upstairs. "That woman had me drive practically to the New York border to drop off her stupid dog. I'll have to get my car professionally cleaned to clear all that hair out."

"What kind of dog?" Maddy asked.

"Oh, I don't know. Big, black, and, well, a dog."

Maddy suppressed a smirk. Jen and animals didn't mix well. Not even Maddy's tortoise that she'd brought with her for this trip. "Well, thank you for bringing Tamar here. It's a great help."

Jen hmphed her way right out the front door, and Maddy laughed to herself. She had no idea why Kenneth kept Jen as his top assistant, but that was his business. Unfortunately, the new guest upstairs was her business now. She should go up and greet her, but she postponed her visit for a few minutes, under the excuse of getting a light snack for herself first.

Kenneth had made his mark in the kitchen. The newly remodeled room glowed with white countertops and steel appliances, a contrast to the rest of the more traditional New England home furnishings. With their parents determined to stay abroad for their retirement, it only made sense that he should change the house to match his tastes, even if he spent most of his time in a condo in Boston. Maddy had preferred the older setting, more comfortable and reminiscent of her childhood.

She made herself a small plate of cheese, crackers, and grapes and eschewed the formal dining room to eat at the kitchen island instead. When she finished cleaning up after herself, she squared her shoulders and prepared to greet her new guest and student. She made her slow way up the stairs and down the corridor. The door to the bedroom stood open.

Maddy peered inside and was about to knock when she saw the form of someone already asleep on the guest bed. Knowing her way around the room, she left her cane in the hallway and quietly slipped inside to find the switch near the bed that lowered the shades. She paused, glancing down at Tamar, who slept fully dressed, from the looks of it, her black, curly hair a halo around her pixie face. Even with just the moon for light, Tamar's lips appeared a bright contrast to her pale features. Maddy smiled, tempted to pull the covers up over Tamar's shoulder, but shook herself out of that urge. What was she thinking, invading a stranger's room?

She flipped the switch and made her way back out. The shades slowly lowered, blocking out the moonlight and the glaring sunlight that would have greeted Tamar around six in the morning if Maddy hadn't lowered them. She shut the door with a quiet click, giving Tamar her privacy. Maddy walked to the adjacent bedroom, formerly the guest room but the one she preferred on her home visits, as it had an attached bathroom. She should stay in her old bedroom at the other end of the hall if she really wanted privacy but didn't have the energy.

Tomorrow would come soon enough. Tonight, Maddy would make good use of that bathroom with a long soak in the old-fashioned claw-foot bathtub.

CHAPTER SIX

The incessant buzzing on her phone woke Tamar up from a deep sleep. Her first conscious thought was to strangle whoever was sending her a steady stream of texts. Her second conscious thought made her sit up and toss the covers off her in the darkened room.

"Where the heck am I?"

She grabbed her phone and read the flood of texts from her cousin Samantha that reminded her of exactly where she was, along with a deep level of snark about it mixed in with real concern. She texted back a yawn emoji.

You woke me up.

Good. Now put your clothes on and leave.

Tamar glanced down at the wrinkled mess of her nursing scrubs. *Already dressed.*

Halfway out the door then.

Tamar yawned, stretched, and shivered. *Your worry is deeply moving.*

Bitch. Nanna called me.

I guessed.

Tamar glanced around, looking for the warm sweater she had on last night. She barely remembered taking it off in the middle of the night and pulling the covers over herself instead.

Glad to hear that gray matter is still working.

Tamar heard someone in the hallway. *Company coming. I'll text you later. I'm fine.*

Fine, my ass. If I don't hear from you in two hours, I'm sending a rescue team.

Tamar chuckled as she put down her phone. The room had an unnatural darkness for what her phone told her was ten in the morning. She flicked on the fancy side lamp and looked around at her new room. It had a pleasant feel, comforting, though a bit too girlie for her tastes.

To her embarrassment, she'd crawled into bed shoes and all. She pulled back the covers to give the sheets a good brush, then made the bed as neatly as she could. She tried to raise the shades on the nearest window but felt a resistance to her pull. However they worked, it was beyond her for the moment.

She was desperate for a shower, but the bandage on her hand made that impossible for now. Instead, she grabbed a bundle of fresh clothes and went in search of the nearest bathroom. She walked down the hallway to the sound of a man's voice and poked her head into the first open doorway on her left. A young man sat in a room that looked more like a nursing station, complete with rolling medical monitors, IV drip, and a laptop he was talking at.

He waved her in, and she sat in a side chair while he finished his video conference. He spoke in Spanish, she guessed, given the little Puerto Rican flag on his desk. He wore light-blue scrubs, wrinkle-free, unlike her own, and sported half his hair as natural black, the other half dyed light gray, all combed up into a peak.

He finished his call. "Sorry about that. You must be Tamar? I'm Luis Moreno, the nurse here."

A house nurse? He held out his hand, and she shook it. "Sorry. I was just looking for the nearest bathroom."

"Yes. It's a big place to get used to. The bathroom is the second door on the left, back the way you came. I wouldn't recommend a shower, though. Given your condition, you should avoid long periods of standing for now."

"You know about my condition?"

"Yes. Kenneth gave me the rundown. Necro fatigue will limit your activity for a while." He smiled. "Think of this as a little vacation. We even have a private beach."

Tamar stood up, feeling a wave of light-headedness that made her want to sit right back down. She steadied herself on the desk as she waited for her full vision to return.

Luis stood up. "Let me take you to the bathroom. When you're done, just give a shout, and I can help you back here to check your dressing."

With his hand on her elbow, he escorted her to the bathroom and thankfully left her on her own. As a nurse, she'd had to help patients of all genders, but at her age she just didn't want to face the idea of being on the opposite end of that situation.

The small bathroom had a porcelain sink and toilet, as well as a small shower, with deep-green decor and matching towels. Tamar took one facecloth and did the best she could with a one-handed sponge bath, sitting on the toilet lid for most of it. Fatigue was nasty.

Feeling moderately better for being clean and dressed, she dumped her dirty scrubs next to her suitcase back in the bedroom. Then she fiddled with switches by the bed until she found one that controlled the shades. Sunlight poured into the room, brightening her spirits.

Luis joined her in the hallway. "Feeling better?"

"Yes, thanks. I'm a nurse, so I can probably take care of my own bandage check."

He smiled. "Don't make me say it…"

She grinned back. "Yeah. Nurses are the worst patients. Okay. Fine."

Luis made quick work of checking the stitches in Tamar's palm. What was she thinking, cutting herself that deeply? He changed the gauze and taped it. "You shouldn't need this after today, but we should still wrap it in plastic if you want to take a bath."

He took her vitals while she sat there. "BP is low, but that's expected. You'll have problems with that for some time, along with general fatigue. For now, I think it best if you sit as much as possible. You won't be able to do anything requiring your full attention for a least a few days."

"As in?" Tamar asked.

"As in no driving or operating heavy equipment." He smiled. "Not that there's any heavy equipment around here. Let me help you downstairs and show you around the kitchen."

Tamar's stomach grumbled its agreement with that suggestion, and with Luis again at her elbow, she walked down the staircase. The first floor had multiple rooms that she glanced into on their way to the back kitchen. Everything looked perfect in a way her apartment never did, and she was glad she'd dropped Kalev off at her grandmother's.

Someone already sat at the kitchen island, an Asian woman with black hair and brown highlights cascading past her shoulders. She turned as Tamar and Luis entered. Tamar flashed a quick memory of seeing her at the hospital, and a blush heated her cheeks.

"This is Dr. Maddy Wu," Luis said.

"Yes. We've met," Maddy said. "Please, have a seat. We have wheat bread for toast, eggs, and yogurt with granola. We can put in a grocery order later today to get whatever food you prefer."

"That's okay," Tamar said. "Yogurt will be fine."

"I can get it for you."

"I'm okay. I can get it if you just point me where things are."

"Fatigue will be with you for a time," Maddy said. "It's okay to accept help."

Tamar didn't understand something in Maddy's steady stare, but she made her own way to the fridge and pulled out a tub of plain vanilla. Maddy went and stood next to her, close enough to return the blush to Tamar's cheeks. Maddy was a good few inches taller than her, and her light-brown skin tone contrasted to

Tamar's paler color as they passed items back and forth to prepare Tamar's breakfast. In the end, she had fresh peaches sliced into her yogurt, with a sprinkle of granola on top for added crunch.

"Thanks," she said.

Maddy cleaned up her own breakfast and put her dishes in the dishwasher. "Not a problem." She turned deep brown eyes at Tamar. "Do you feel up for joining me in the sunroom after breakfast? We can go over the next steps."

With a mouthful of yogurt, Tamar just nodded. She hoped by the time she finished eating, she'd get over her silly blushing and be able to have a coherent conversation. Which would be harder in the next few weeks—preparing for and passing her necromancy licensing exam or not making a fool of herself in front of a beautiful woman?

Of course she already knew the answer. Tamar and goober went hand in hand when it came to women. She kept her eyes on her food as Maddy left the kitchen.

❖

Maddy sat in the sunroom again with a steaming mug of fresh coffee and her cane tucked away beside the sofa. She placed her head in her hands for a moment to compose herself. Tamar would be here in a few moments, and Maddy needed to think clearly when she arrived. Maddy's wayward thoughts kept returning to the cute blushes that colored Tamar's cheeks as they'd prepared breakfast together. Maddy knew Tamar didn't need her help, but she couldn't bring herself to step away.

That sort of distraction was the last thing Maddy needed, not with the House committee hearings going on and her research in a critical stage. When she agreed to take on Tamar as an informal student, she'd never considered her own physical attraction to the other woman would be an issue.

She was a Wu. She could handle this.

By the time Maddy heard the sounds of Tamar's approach,

she'd gotten herself back under control. She took a long sip of her coffee and resisted the urge to watch Tamar enter the room.

"That's an amazing view," Tamar said as she dropped onto the sofa at the opposite end from Maddy.

"It was our parents' house," Maddy said. "They were lawyers specializing in private equity for years."

"Are they okay with me staying here?"

"They've been traveling the world for the past five years. They transferred the house to me and Kenneth over a year ago."

Tamar sat with one hand covering her bandaged one, taking in the broad expanse of ocean view from the sunroom's windows.

Maddy pointed at Tamar's hand. "Let's start with that. Can you explain why you cut yourself?"

Tamar shrugged. "Nerves, I guess. I knew my blood could help the accident victim, and I didn't think an ambulance would get there in time. The person had no pulse."

Maddy nodded. "So you already knew you were a necromancer."

"Yes. Untrained, though. My grandmother has issues with necromancy."

Maddy thought of Jasmine at the statehouse. "Yes. Many people do."

"It's not like that," Tamar said. "My grandmother isn't against necromancy itself. She's more concerned with how quickly society can change its views. She's a professor emeritus at Clark University, specializing in Jewish philosophy."

Maddy raised an eyebrow. "That's impressive."

"Yeah." Tamar smirked. "Try growing up under that kind of attention. Basically, she's afraid what was legalized can be made illegal just as quickly, and the prejudice against our kind will come back with a vengeance."

Maddy wanted to ask why Tamar was raised by her grandmother but decided that question crossed the professional boundary she needed to keep in place between them. "Your grandmother has a valid point. Still, you should have gotten some basic training in high school."

Tamar raised her good hand. "Homeschooled."

Maddy took a sip of coffee while she let that information settle. She'd have to start with the basics, which made her job that much harder. "What do you know about necromancy?"

"Not much. I know it's based on blood."

"Actually, saliva can work as well, though not as strong. You know, like Jesus using spit to heal."

Tamar raised a hand again. "Jewish, remember? I didn't spend a lot of time learning what Jesus did or didn't do with his bodily fluids."

Maddy chuckled.

"Oh, you have dimples," Tamar said.

Maddy again escaped to her coffee to hide her blush. She put her mug down when she felt she had herself under control again. "As I said, saliva and blood both work, but blood is stronger. It's also easier to control the dosage. That's possibly why you're suffering from necromantic fatigue. The uncontrolled dose you administered put too much of your life energy into the person you resurrected."

"Life energy?" Tamar asked.

Maddy winced. "Yes. We don't have a better term for it yet. My own research is attempting to isolate what's in the blood of a necromancer that provides that healing property. For now, most people know it as life energy, so that's the term we use until we can come up with a scientific basis for what's happening."

Tamar looked at her hand. "So next time, less a knife cut, more a pinprick?"

Maddy frowned. "Next time, you'll be licensed and have measured doses of your blood available. Either a full dose, based on your own blood's necromantic strength, or partial doses if you choose to work with deathbed depositions."

Tamar grimaced. "That sounds macabre."

"It's not for the faint of heart. But since it's not a full resurrection, it's not like the person is alive. And it only happens under a court order. As part of your training, you'll get to experience one yourself. Also, while this is not officially required, someone with your skill should really consider becoming a resurrector. We have a shortage of those, nationwide."

"My grandmother thinks my mom might have been a resurrector. That was before it was all legalized."

Tamar looked down at her hands but didn't elaborate. Maddy feared she'd hit some sort of nerve and wanted to ask but, again, pulled back from that instinct. Best to stay professional as much as possible. She glanced at the wall clock. "It's nearing noon. I need to go to the lab for a time. We can start your training tomorrow."

Tamar glanced up. "Any chance you want company? I'm not used to just sitting around all day."

"You'd likely be bored there as well." Something in Tamar's eyes softened Maddy's stance. "But you're welcome to come along. I'll call an Uber."

"I think your brother's assistant brought my car here. Luis says I can't drive yet, but you're welcome to drive if you want."

Maddy picked up her cane and stood. "I don't drive. We'll leave in thirty minutes."

❖

Tamar slid into the back seat of the Uber next to Maddy. "Sorry about earlier."

Maddy glanced at her. "About what?"

"About the driving thing. I didn't know."

"No reason you should."

Tamar thought Maddy might elaborate, but they settled into an awkward silence instead for the short ride to Maddy's lab. The drive ended with a loop around a small pond with a handful of young trees and stopped in front of the Conn Biotech main office building. Maddy led the way in, getting a guest badge for Tamar and proceeding up the elevator to the fourth floor.

"That's an amazing view," Tamar said as they stepped out of the elevator.

Maddy glanced out the floor-to-ceiling windows that looked over that pond and its surrounding landscaped walkways. "Yes. I suppose it is."

They walked around to the left and eventually into a small window office, where Maddy sat and pulled out her laptop. Tamar took the second chair and continued to look out the window, wondering why she'd come. Well, not wondering too much, since Maddy was an expert in all things necromancy-related. Tamar felt like she'd burst if she didn't start asking questions, but just as she was about to blurt out the first one, Maddy closed her laptop.

"Are you interested in becoming part of a necromancy study?" Maddy asked. "I have a state grant to delve into the relative differences between resurrectors and deathbed depositioners and could use another resurrector test subject."

"There's a difference? I thought it was just a matter of how much blood was used," Tamar said.

"That's the common understanding, but I think there is a difference. We know most necromancers actually can't resurrect at all, and those who can vary in how it impacts them."

Tamar couldn't stifle a yawn. "Like necromantic fatigue?" She really could just crawl back into bed, given the opportunity.

Maddy nodded. "Among other things, yes."

"Sure. I'm up for it. What do I have to do?"

"Nothing difficult. I just need a few blood samples." Maddy smiled, showing her dimples again, and Tamar's heart almost melted. She looked away as her blush crawled up her neck as a dead giveaway. Stupid blood vessels betraying her again.

Maddy led the way to her lab, a bright room with sparkling lab benches and equipment that Tamar couldn't fathom except for the obvious microscopes. Before they entered, Maddy gave her a face mask and gloves. "To prevent cross-contamination."

Tamar obliged, and they sat at a lab bench that held multiple vials of what looked like blood, along with a handful of fancy plastic things. Tamar pointed to one. "What are these?"

"Necromantic injectors. You'll use them once you're licensed so you can give a strict measured dose, depending on resurrection or deposition."

Maddy pulled out a needle and vials, and futzed with the lab computer. A printer under the bench came to life, spitting out a series of labels with Tamar's information on it. Was it odd that Maddy already had all of Tamar's details in her system? She kept her paranoia to herself, knowing it reflected her upbringing and her grandmother's antigovernment feelings more than any of her own. Nanna had a strict don't-let-them-track-you attitude that didn't acknowledge they already tracked you if you did anything online anyway.

Maddy peeled off each sticker and labeled three vials. "Are you okay with needles?"

Tamar nodded and pulled up her sleeve with her one good hand. With expert care, Maddy prepared the site and then inserted the needle. Tamar ignored the pinch and waited as Maddy filled all three vials.

"This first step is obvious, but we need to go through it anyway." Maddy picked up a pipette and put samples of Tamar's blood into a small tray. "Each sample includes partially decayed material. Your blood will revive each of them."

"Can I see it?"

Maddy put the first tray under the microscope and set a timer. "Here you go. It will take thirty seconds before you see results."

Tamar focused the microscope on the sample tray. At first, she could see little activity, but seconds later she let out a shout. "There it is! I can see the cell life regenerating."

She looked up at Maddy, who looked back at her with a frown. "May I?"

Tamar stepped away from the microscope, and Maddy took

over. "Yes. You're right." Maddy looked at her timer, which still had fifteen seconds left. "Let me try this again."

Tamar sat still while Maddy reran the test on a new test tray. This time Maddy started a timer at zero. At the ten-second mark, she stopped it. "That's interesting."

"What is?" Tamar asked.

Maddy looked at her and then back at the microscope. "It's possible this is a side effect of using fresh blood. Most of my test samples have been stored for at least a few hours." She looked back at Tamar. "Congratulations. You're a necromancer." She smiled again, something Tamar could get used to seeing.

"Thanks." Tamar yawned again.

"I can store your samples to process further another day. It's time you went back home to rest."

"I'm okay," Tamar said, forcing her vision into focus again.

Maddy laid a warm hand on her forearm. "Necromantic fatigue needs time. Trust me. You don't want to push yourself this early."

Tamar glanced down where Maddy's hand rested and felt a warmth travel farther than that one connection. Maddy took away her hand, and Tamar looked up to see Maddy's cheeks flushed.

"I'll be right back," Maddy said.

Tamar sat on the lab stool to wait. She didn't have much interest in the lab equipment, but she picked up one of the injectors. It had a white base, with a red-tinged window and yellow flared tip for the needle and a button on the other end. Maddy entered the lab again as she examined the injector. She was about to ask a question about it when she felt a familiar jolt of energy flood back into her system. She couldn't stop the gasp that escaped from her lips.

Maddy grabbed the injector pen out of her hand. "Shit. What did you do?"

Tamar closed her eyes, wanting a moment to acknowledge the passing of her hospice patient, Janice, but Maddy grabbed her wrist.

"You juiced yourself, didn't you? I can't frigging believe I trusted you." Maddy pushed all the injector pens out of Tamar's reach.

Tamar frowned. "What are you talking about?"

"I've been in the necromancy world longer than you have, and I recognize the signs of someone feeding off necromantic energy."

Tamar held up her hands. "I don't know what you're accusing me of, but I didn't do anything with your precious injector pen. Look at it."

"And yet here you are, full of energy when you were ready to fall asleep before I left the lab."

❖

Maddy was furious. This was all Kenneth's fault. Bad enough he'd saddled her with what amounted to private tutoring of a complete stranger, but now an untrustworthy one at that. And to think she'd blushed at their shared contact a few moments earlier. *Pulled in by a cute smile and beautiful brown eyes.*

"I wouldn't call this full of energy," Tamar said with a sigh. "But yes, I did just get a jolt, as you call it. Not from one of those pens, though."

"Then how do you explain it?" Maddy asked, examining each of her pens. To her surprise, they all remained unused.

"Look," Tamar said. "I know it's not strictly legal, but I've been using my blood to help my hospice patients last that little bit longer." She looked out the window. "No one should ever be kept from saying good-bye to a loved one."

Maddy folded her arms. "Just how many laws do you break on a regular basis?"

Tamar winced. "Okay, maybe I deserve that, but that's what I'm here for, right? To learn and be licensed so I'm not breaking any laws anymore."

Maddy fiddled with one of the injector pens, wondering how

much she should trust Tamar. She must be telling the truth because the pens were safe. Maddy wanted to call out Tamar's reckless behavior but held her tongue. "Since you're more energetic, I'd like to rerun the vitals tests Luis did earlier. We can compare the impact of that returned necromantic energy to your earlier stats."

"It's Janice's death," Tamar said.

Maddy frowned. "Excuse me?"

"What you clinically call returned necromantic energy. It means my hospice patient, Janice, has passed away." *May her memory be a blessing.*

"Oh. Yes. Sorry." Maddy silently kicked herself for being so cold. Not for the first time, she wished she had Luis's knack for empathy. "We don't have to run the tests. We don't have baseline data anyway to understand the level of necromantic transference you gave your patient. I mean, Janice."

"One milliliter, given orally."

"That's rather precise," Maddy said.

Tamar smiled. "I've been doing this for a bit, so I learned what works and what doesn't."

"And by doesn't, you mean the patient passes anyway?"

"More like I erred on the opposite side. My first patient lasted another six months. I had to call in sick for a week after that, because I just couldn't get out of bed."

Maddy frowned. "Only a week? Your recuperative skills are impressive. Raising someone whose body was failing from sickness or age takes considerable necromantic energy."

"Not sure it's something I should feel proud about, but I learned after that to limit what I give."

"Except at the accident scene."

Tamar nodded. "Hard to measure a jagged cut."

Maddy stood. "Well, we can measure vitals here. Let's see what's changed."

She led Tamar into a side room, where her lab assistants took down the basics from each volunteer in their clinical study. She directed Tamar to hop onto the exam table.

"I don't have to put on a paper Jonny, do I?" Tamar asked with a grin.

Maddy smiled back. "No, but I will want to do some more blood-pressure tests, beyond what Luis did this morning."

As Tamar sat quietly, Maddy took BP readings from both arms while she sat, stood, and lay back on the exam table. Maddy sat at her computer to create a new file for Tamar and note the results.

"If you agree, we'll draw blood next," Maddy said.

"Agree? Um, sure."

Maddy swiveled her chair to look at Tamar. "You're a necromancer. You should never give blood without fully understanding where and how it will be used."

Tamar frowned down at her. "You mean people would actually steal my blood?"

"Once training officially starts, you'll be registered as a necromancer in the state database, so yes, there is the potential for someone to steal your blood."

Tamar hid a yawn behind her hand. "Nanna's going to flip."

"Nanna?" Maddy asked.

"My grandmother. Reason number one I'm a closet necromancer. No offense, but she doesn't trust the government to hold that kind of information. We're Jewish, so government registration to isolate one type of person from another? Yeah. She's going to flip."

"I hadn't really considered that response." Maddy had always assumed government registration helped necromancers by making them eligible for training assistance and health care. "How do you feel about it?"

Tamar shrugged. "I'm not excited about it, to be honest. But I am glad to have the chance to train and become licensed."

Maddy turned back to her computer and sent a file to the printer. She handed it to Tamar with a pen. "This is a blood-release form. From now on, whenever you have a blood test, you'll want to sign this form. Even at your doctor's office. The one doctors or hospitals have strictly prohibits any other use of your blood beyond whatever tests they are running. This form is a little different. It releases your blood to Conn Biotech for specific tests and mandates that this facility correctly dispose of the rest. It also forms a legal liability with the facility should your blood end up used for any other purposes."

"Including theft?" Tamar asked as she read the form and signed it.

"Including theft. Massachusetts has some of the best legal protections for necromancers in the nation, but that varies state by state. And with states that have no protections, necromancers have gotten severely ill after their blood was used without their approval."

"Used for?" Tamar asked.

"Juicing and age rejuvenation are the most common. There's a black market in necromantic blood that's growing in some states. That's one of the reasons Kenneth has his eyes set on higher office. He wants to take the protections in Massachusetts to the federal level."

"Well, that makes me like him better," Tamar said.

Maddy raised an eyebrow. "Better?"

Tamar's eyes widened. "I mean I like him, for sure. I just meant, well, you know, he's fighting the good fight, right?"

Maddy stifled a laugh. Tamar was cute when she became flustered. "I get it. Let's start the blood draws."

"Multiple?"

"Multiple. One sitting. Then I'll ask you to stand for fifteen minutes, and I'll draw the second set. We're looking for the markers that might show where changes occur in your fatigue levels."

Tamar waited patiently for the first draw and stood for her fifteen minutes for the second as Maddy filled out her reports and prepped the vials for tests that her lab assistants would do for her later.

With all tests done and recorded, Maddy grabbed her cane

and stood. She bent down to rub her knees, not that it would help the aching much.

"You okay?" Tamar asked, pulling on her yellow sweater.

"Yes. It's just the weather. I'm sure it's raining outside by now."

Tamar glanced down. "Your knees are barometers?"

Maddy turned away. "Something like that."

CHAPTER SEVEN

Tamar spent the next week taking more online training modules than she'd done since she got her nursing license. Some of it was interesting, like the future research modules and the history modules. Others were dull as dirt when it came to all the safety regulations, codes of conduct, and other modules that seemed more focused on legalities than the real-world aspects of being a licensed necromancer.

Her energy levels improved some over the week, but she still had to nap most afternoons and couldn't even think of taking up jogging again. According to Luis and Maddy, she might not reach her prior fitness level for a year or more. That fact, more than anything, brought home the risk she'd taken with the accident victim.

Still, the first occurrences of crispness in the air called to her, and she spent as much time as possible walking along the sandy beach behind what she started calling the Wu mansion. She was sitting in the cool sand watching the Atlantic waves lap along the shore when her phone buzzed.

"Hi, Samantha," she said.

"When are you leaving that prison?"

Tamar looked back at the large yellow home behind her and the forested hill that blocked out the setting sun. "Hardly a prison. And I told you, not for a month at least. They say it'll take that long for the fatigue to stabilize."

She didn't like that they called it stabilizing instead of going away entirely, but she had only herself to blame for that one.

"Nanna's having a fit," Samantha said.

Tamar laughed. "Nanna's too philosophical for fits."

"She stepped down from the town historical committee."

"Nanna's pushing eighty. Maybe she just wanted a break."

"From waxing on about the origins of this and that?" Samantha said.

Tamar picked up a stone and tried skipping it into the surf. It landed with a thud that couldn't even count for one hop. "Fine. I'll call her."

"And tell her when you're leaving."

"Samantha, I don't know when I'm leaving."

"Tamar Marilyn Richler. You're being deliberately vague. It's almost as if you don't want to get back to your life."

Tamar couldn't stop the image of Maddy from coming to mind, and she thanked her lucky star this beach didn't have a strong enough cell phone signal for a video-based call. She could feel the heat rising in her cheeks.

"Tamar?"

"Um, yeah. No. I'm cool." She winced at her own fumbling.

"You have a crush on her, don't you?"

"Who?" If Tamar's cheeks felt any hotter, she'd have to dunk her head in the ocean to cool them off.

Samantha snorted. "You know exactly who I'm talking about. That teacher of yours. I looked her up, you know. She's just your type, with that long hair and those flashy eyes."

"Flashy eyes don't come across in a picture, Samantha."

"You're not denying they are flashy, though, are you?"

Dang if her cousin didn't have her pegged. "Fine. Yes. She's attractive. But put your mind at rest. She hasn't been here most of the week. I get messages from her on what training to take next."

Tamar hoped her disappointment didn't show in her voice. Maddy was beautiful in the most unattainable sort of way. She hadn't even determined if the woman liked women or not. Maybe she could eke that information out of Luis one of these days.

"Anyway, Luis here is the person I talk to most, and even you know my gate doesn't swing that way."

"Is he the brother?" Samantha asked.

"No. He's the nurse who takes care of the other brother, the one in a coma."

"Oh, that's sad. How long's he been that way?"

Tamar worked her fingers into the cold sand. "I don't know. They don't talk much about him. I haven't even met him yet."

"See? Something weird going on up there, and you need to leave."

Tamar laughed, again. "What would I do without your overactive paranoia, cousin?"

"Probably get sucked into some vortex of necromantic hell. Seriously, though, watch out for yourself. And it wouldn't hurt you to call Nanna some more. She really is worried in her own stoic way."

"Yes. I will. I should get back, though. I promised Luis I'd toast him at *Power Nexus* tonight."

"You and your video games. Go. Call Nanna."

Tamar pocketed her phone, trying not to smile. She stood, brushed the sand off her jeans, and headed to the house. As she walked up the granite steps to the back of the house, the track lights flickered on across the gravel path. She took off her sneakers in the sunroom, not that anyone told her to keep shoes off in the house, but it just seemed a place not to tread dirt into.

After a week, she knew her way around most of the common rooms on the first floor, including the way to what she called the green room—a room painted floor to ceiling in light green, with built-in bookshelves lining two of the four walls. The third wall had windows out to the front gravel drive, and the fourth had the large-screen TV they played their games on.

Luis already sat in the only non-green piece of furniture in the room and patted the seat next to him on the darker-green sofa. "Ready to get beat again?" he asked.

"I think if you check, I won the last two games," she said, plopping down next to him and grabbing the second controller.

"An anomaly. I won the first five."

Luis wore his usual nursing scrubs, no matter the time of day. She thought he might even sleep in them, given she'd never seen him in anything else. But then, this was both his job and his home, so why shouldn't he be casual?

As usual, Tamar lost herself in the game, sometimes advancing beyond Luis, but most times falling behind. She was almost glad when she heard the crunch of gravel and a car's headlights flash across the semidark room.

Because she hadn't seen Kenneth since that first day, she assumed it was Maddy. The red rear lights of the car turning back down the drive confirmed it.

"Maddy never drives?" she asked.

"Never. Her injuries happened before she was old enough to learn, and, well, she's been head-down in her research ever since, from what their former nurse told me."

Luis could be trusted to bring out a bit of family gossip now and then, but Tamar didn't push it. If Maddy wanted her to know the full story, she'd tell her. Sooner or later.

Maybe?

Meanwhile, Tamar did her best to push her unruly curls back in place, ignoring Luis's smirk. It disappeared when they both heard the distinctive click of Maddy's cane on the wood floors.

"Must have been a hard day," he said, handing Tamar the controller. He stood up and looked back at her. "Doesn't mean you win this round."

Tamar looked at the score on the screen, with his nearly double hers. "We'll call it a tie."

He snorted as he left to help Maddy.

Tamar took another moment to straighten out her sweatshirt and contemplated going upstairs to change into something more presentable, but that would just confirm Luis's suspicion of her crush, and she didn't need that level of ribbing just now. Instead, she looked one last time at her reflection in the now-turned-off TV and went to greet her host.

❖

Maddy rested her cane on the edge of the dark-wood side table and collapsed onto the cream sofa in the main living room. Her eyes drifted shut as she leaned her head back, but the sound of both Luis and Tamar heading her way made her sit up again.

"Long day?" Luis asked as he came in with a glass of lemon water and handed it to her.

"Thanks." She took a long sip. "Long week. I'm being summoned once again by the Most Honorable Representative I-Hate-Necromancers."

Luis chuckled. "Bunte could try the patience of a saint."

Maddy saw Tamar standing in the doorway as if hesitant to join them. Maddy took her in, with her tight jeans and sweatshirt bearing the name of yet another sports team Maddy had never heard of. Their gaze locked for a moment, and Maddy lost whatever she was about to say next.

Luis interrupted the awkward moment with a small cough.

Maddy surreptitiously straightened out her light-blue blouse while she tried to regain her focus.

"Which team is that?" Maddy asked, pointing at Tamar's dayglow green sweatshirt.

Tamar glanced down. "Oh, this one is Wolfsburg. Women's soccer team in Germany."

Maddy nodded. "So that makes Germany, the US, and England. Any other countries you follow?"

"Oh, they're not the national teams. Just their professional women's soccer teams. And no. I think that's about it. Though there's a really good player on one of the English teams that's Irish, so you never know."

Maddy smiled. "Must be missing something. I haven't seen any of these. Or any soccer since my brothers played in high school."

Tamar took a tentative step into the room. "We could watch a game if you're interested. The US league is in their finals, and the European ones are just starting up, so there's almost always a game or two to see on the weekends."

Maddy leaned her head back against the sofa. "Maybe."

"Maybe you need some rest," Luis said.

Maddy looked back up. "Aye, aye, captain. But I have some good news first." She turned back to Tamar. "Come, sit."

Tamar joined her on the sofa and waited.

Maddy pulled a file from her day bag and slipped out a piece of paper that she handed to Tamar. "Congratulations. You're officially an apprentice necromancer in the commonwealth of Massachusetts."

Tamar's lips parted, and she stared down at the paper in her hand, scanning the document with its official seal and Kenneth's signature scrawled across the bottom. With a "woot," Tamar wrapped her arms around Maddy and pulled her into a hug.

"Thanks! Thanks so much," she whispered into Maddy's ear, sending a shiver through Maddy. She wrapped her free arm around Tamar's waist, wishing she weren't still holding the lemon water in her other hand. Tamar's body warmth heated her in ways she didn't quite want to admit to, and definitely not in front of Luis's knowing smirk.

He slipped the glass out of her hand, but she didn't dare prolong the contact with Tamar. She knew her cheeks were as flushed as Tamar's when they separated, but she doubted she looked even half as cute as Tamar did.

"Um, you're quite welcome," she said as Tamar sat back on the sofa. "Your online training scores were excellent. We can start your apprenticeship whenever you feel ready."

Tamar practically bounced in the seat, her blush fading as she stared at her new certificate. "Can we start this weekend?"

Luis held up a hand before Maddy had a chance to agree. "Maybe on Monday. Nurse's orders. You both could do with a relaxing weekend at home. Take in one of those soccer games," he said with a wink at Maddy.

Some people are too observant for their own good, she thought.

Tamar glanced at Maddy. "Oh. Right." She gave what seemed a fake yawn. "You're right. Monday will be soon enough. If you have the time?"

Maddy nodded with a smile. "Yes. I have the time. I've cleared my work calendar for the week."

Tamar's eyes widened, and her grin went from ear to ear. "Great. That's great."

"Yes, great," Luis said. Maddy wanted to smack him for mimicking, and she was surprised when Tamar did, with a light tap to his arm.

"Nobody likes a smart-aleck."

Luis just laughed. "Well, I'll leave you to it. I need to do my night check on Aiden."

As he left, Maddy saw Tamar glancing at the ceiling as if trying to see through to where Maddy's brother lay.

"Something on your mind?" Maddy asked.

Tamar jumped ever so slightly. "Oh, sorry. No. I mean, um…"

Maddy smiled. "It's okay. Ask."

Tamar turned to her. "Aiden. He's Kenneth's twin?"

"Yes."

"And he's been in a coma for some time?"

Maddy's smile slipped. "Fourteen years."

"Oh. Sorry. That must be hard."

"He's family. And we remain hopeful." Even though it was hard sometimes.

The conversation dwindled until Tamar stood. "I should go call Nanna. She likes to hear from me on Friday evenings after she lights the Sabbath candle."

Maddy watched her leave, taking in those tight-fitting jeans before their owner disappeared down the hallway. *You really need to get a grip on yourself, woman. She is your student now.*

She couldn't stop her smile from spreading, nor the anticipation of getting to spend more time with Tamar over the next few weeks. Being a necromancer mentor had its perks.

❖

Tamar yawned so wide during her Sabbath call that her grandmother ended it early, insisting Tamar's jaw would pop off if she didn't get some sleep. Still, Tamar wasn't ready to give up on the day at only eight o'clock in the evening. She stepped out of what she was already calling her room to the soft melody of a flute. She followed the sound to the one room she hadn't stepped into yet, Aiden's room.

Unsure of her welcome, she only peeked into the open doorway. To her surprise, a warm fire crackled in the small fireplace opposite a wide bed, where a lone figure lay covered in a gray-striped comforter. Maddy sat in a chair pulled up next to the bed, her eyes shut as she played the melody on her flute. Tamar couldn't pull herself away from the scene. It seemed beautiful and melancholy at the same time.

She didn't notice the end of the tune until Maddy's eyes drifted open. "Oh, sorry, didn't mean to intrude," Tamar said. "It was just…It's a lovely tune."

Maddy gave her a soft smile as she lowered the flute to her lap. "Aiden wrote it when he was only sixteen." She looked down. "It's his flute as well. I took lessons after the accident, but I don't have near the talent he has."

Tamar noticed the present tense Maddy used with regard to Aiden, and as a hospice nurse, she understood Maddy hadn't given up on him. She glanced at the figure on the bed and could easily recognize the resemblance to Kenneth. The man in the bed had his same features, but thinner and clean-shaven.

"You can come in. Have you met Aiden yet?" Maddy asked.

Tamar stepped into the room, shoving her hands into her jeans pockets. "Um, no."

Maddy turned to her brother. "Aiden, this is Tamar. She's a newly apprenticed necromancer and will be training with us soon."

Tamar felt less awkward now, settling into the familiar routine she'd experienced with some of her own patients' families. "Nice to meet you, Aiden. I like the clean shave. Makes you more handsome than your brother."

Maddy laughed. "I think so too, but Kenneth doesn't believe he should take fashion advice from a lesbian."

Chock that up as one question answered, Tamar thought. "Well, I guess Aiden shouldn't take my advice for the same reason, then."

Did Maddy's eye contact with her after that statement last a bit longer than normal?

"Do you play for him often?" Tamar asked.

"When I can. I confess, I know only a handful of tunes at this point, but I play his composition at least once a visit here."

"That's cool. What about Kenneth? Does he play as well?"

Maddy put the flute back in its black case. "He used to play the violin, but he stopped after the accident."

Tamar bucked up the courage to ask the obvious. "How did it happen?"

Maddy glanced out the window. "They were seventeen and always competitive, at least as long as I can remember. Maybe twins are always that way?"

Tamar didn't think so, but she kept her thoughts to herself.

"Our parents were off in Boston for Labor Day weekend. The remnants of a hurricane were coming up the coast. Aiden challenged Kenneth to surf the waves with him." Maddy placed a hand on Aiden's arm. "He was always the more aggressive of the two. I don't know why Kenneth went along with Aiden's schemes. He seemed to be breaking out on his own more, ignoring Aiden's taunts, but not this time."

"What happened?" Tamar asked.

Maddy turned to her. "Aiden's surfboard slammed down on his head after a huge wave came in. It must have been six feet or more. Kenneth paddled out to help him. I was watching from the shoreline and couldn't do a thing. By the time he dragged Aiden to the shore, he'd stopped breathing."

"How old were you?"

"Fourteen."

Tamar could see the strain this story had on Maddy. She tried to redirect the conversation. "You both did what you could and still are. He's lucky to have you two as family."

Maddy wiped at her eyes and looked at her watch. "Thanks. It's getting late."

Tamar stood up straight. "Yeah. Bedtime comes early for me as well these days."

Maddy walked toward her with a slight smile. "It should pass for you. Just give it some time."

❖

To her chagrin, Maddy spent most of Saturday in bed. She slept until two in the afternoon, then returned for an early evening nap that turned into another full night of sleep, not waking until Sunday morning. The cloud of fatigue had barely lifted, but the aches in her joints forced her out of bed anyway. When raising the blinds, she wasn't surprised to see rain coming down in sheets outside her second-story bedroom window. She lingered for a moment to take in the rough waves crashing on their usually serene beach.

Dressed finally in comfortable cream slacks and her favorite avocado-striped sweater, she headed downstairs with her cane in hand. She paused at the top of the steps as Luis appeared from Aiden's room as if he had a tracker on her.

"Rough morning?" he asked.

"I've had better."

He took her cane and stepped in front of her on the stairs. "Let's take it slow."

Grateful she didn't have to ask for assistance, she placed one hand on the banister and the other on his shoulder for support as they went one step at a time down the stairs. Kenneth kept urging her to convert one of the downstairs rooms into a bedroom, but her stubborn pride wasn't ready for that yet. Her own apartment had no stairs, so she insisted on keeping the upstairs bedroom here until, well, until it wasn't possible for her to climb up and down anymore.

At the base of them she took her cane back. "Thank you. And what's that delicious smell?"

"Tamar is making some kind of Jewish breakfast dish. For you," he said.

This time, Maddy did give him a light slap.

"Seriously. I heard her get the recipe from her grandmother on the phone last night. You're lucky. It could have been chicken soup made with a whole chicken."

Maddy laughed despite her embarrassment as they made their way into the kitchen. The room was transformed from its usual pristine condition to a whirlwind of activity and, frankly, messiness.

Tamar turned from the stove with a broad smile. "Perfect timing! This will be ready in a minute. Luis says you like eggs."

Tamar had on an apron that Maddy hadn't seen since their parents moved away, and it was covered in flour, which also appeared on Tamar's cheek. Resisting the urge to brush it off with her own fingers, Maddy instead pointed. "You have a little bit of something, right here."

"Oh," Tamar pulled up the edge of the apron and wiped. "Better?"

Maddy smiled, taking a seat at the table. "Yes. You didn't have to cook for me, though."

"My treat," Tamar said. To Maddy's surprise, she brought over the entire cast-iron frying pan and placed it on a trivet

Maddy didn't even know they owned. Tamar pulled off the apron and left it on the counter, returning with a basket of fresh-baked wheat bread, and sat opposite Maddy.

"So this is shakshuka. It's an Israeli dish my grandmother picked up when she lived there for a few years."

Maddy inhaled the scent coming off the pan that held cooked diced tomatoes and onions with four poached eggs in the center. Sprigs of fresh parsley were sprinkled across the top. "It smells delicious."

Tamar grinned as she scooped out a serving and handed it to Maddy in a shallow bowl. "Bread?"

"Yes, please. I can't believe you did all this."

Tamar shrugged. "My grandmother's idea. She thinks food is the cure for all ailments." She blushed. "Sorry. I just meant…"

Maddy smiled. "No need to apologize. On a day like today, I'll try any cures your grandmother might suggest." She took her first spoonful and closed her eyes. "Especially ones that taste this good."

After Luis returned upstairs, brunch continued, with Tamar filling Maddy in on her grandmother's history, from her time in New York, to a few years on a kibbutz in Israel while she got her PhD in Jewish philosophy before returning to the States and getting married.

"Sorry to hear that your mother died when you were only ten," Maddy said after Tamar finished with that detail of her childhood. "That must have been hard."

Tamar looked off into the distance. "It was a long illness. We had time to prepare."

Maddy didn't think any amount of time could prepare a child for losing her parent, but she didn't want to push. "Thank you again for such a delicious meal. I owe you one."

The smile returned to Tamar's lips, lips Maddy spent too much time looking at. "Then I'm cashing in that payback. There's an Arsenal women's soccer game on in ten minutes. Are you up for watching?"

Maddy couldn't help but laugh. "Sure."

"Green room or yellow?" Tamar asked as she put the remnants of brunch into containers in the fridge and left the pan to soak in the sink.

"Excuse me?"

Tamar turned to her. "There are TVs in the room painted all green or in the room painted yellow."

"Oh, the green room is my mother's library. The yellow one is where I usually watch TV." Not that she watched much, but a soccer game could be interesting, at least with Tamar explaining things along the way. Maddy stood with her cane and made her way into the "yellow" room with a smile.

Tamar joined her a moment later. "Mind if I take control?"

Maddy's mind went to places that had nothing to do with TV controls, and she inhaled quickly to bring her wayward thoughts back in line. "Please."

Tamar flipped channels faster than Maddy could keep track of, but she ended on one of the sports channels. "It's Arsenal versus Reading. They actually played earlier today, but at like seven in the morning our time. Won't be a fair match, but still fun."

"Why not fair?" Maddy asked.

"Arsenal is at the top of their game. Reading just moved up from the Championship league."

Maddy nodded as if she understood. Tamar continued with explaining the top players on each team in more depth than she could ever imagine. "You really know your players."

Tamar grinned and looked at her from under dark eyelashes. "Yeah. I probably spend too much time following them all on social media and whatnot."

Maddy laughed. "I can think of worse hobbies."

"Such as?" Tamar asked in a teasing tone.

"Oh, I don't dare confess."

Tamar gave Maddy a mischievous grin. "Now I have to know. What's your secret hobby?"

"Well, it's not that secret, but it is silly."

Tamar watched her with wide brown eyes until Maddy confessed. "I make soaps."

"Soaps."

"Soaps," Maddy said. "It's kind of fun."

"Like the decorative soaps in the bathrooms here? Are they yours?"

Maddy cringed. "Yes. If you can't foist your hobbies on family, who can you foist them on?"

Tamar rested a hand on Maddy's elbow. "But those are fantastic! I didn't want to use them the first night because they looked too pretty. Luis said they were meant to be used, but he never said you made them."

Maddy felt the warmth of Tamar's hand on her arm as she smiled. "Thanks. Glad you like them. And they are meant to be used. When I get in a mood, I can produce dozens of them. Someone has to start using them."

Tamar gave her a mock salute. "I volunteer. They have the best scents."

Meanwhile, the announcer on the TV became exceptionally excited, and so did Tamar when she turned back. With a leap, she clapped in celebration.

"I take it that's your team?"

Tamar nodded. "Arsenal all the way, baby."

Maddy wasn't much of a sports person, but watching Tamar watch her favorite team win looked to be a perfect way to spend a rainy Sunday afternoon.

CHAPTER EIGHT

I'm fine to drive," Tamar said. "Ask Luis."

"Do you really want to drive into Boston traffic?" Maddy sipped her morning coffee, not making eye contact with Tamar. "I'm used to taking an Uber."

Tamar still didn't know the full story on Maddy's odd refusal to drive, but she didn't want to push that button this morning. "Boston traffic isn't so bad."

Maddy looked up at her, and Tamar grinned. "Well, mostly not that bad. Still, I haven't gotten behind the wheel in ages. It'll be fun."

Maddy finished her coffee and put the mug in the dishwasher. "You have an unusual definition of the word fun."

Tamar's grin widened. "That means yes, doesn't it?"

Maddy shook her head with a smile of her own starting. "Yes, fine. You can drive us. But I don't want to hear cursing when we hit the expressway."

"Promise. No cursing." Tamar gave a woot and hugged Maddy by the sink, an unnecessary hug, but she got away with them under the guise of friendliness. Also, they just felt good. Minutes later, she held open the door to her Jeep so Maddy could slip into the passenger seat.

"It's a vivid orange," Maddy said as Tamar slid in on her side and started the engine.

"Makes it easy to find in a parking lot."

As they eased onto the highway, Maddy turned off the car radio. "Since this is your first deathbed deposition, let's review a few things."

"Oh. Pop-quiz time?" Tamar asked.

Maddy laughed. "Since you put it that way, then yes. Question one—explain the precursor to any deposition."

"It's done only under a court order, and only if the deceased has allowed for it in their will. After the...the...Okay. I can't remember the specific bill number, but what we call the Bill of Rights for the Deceased states that even in death, an individual is protected by the right to privacy unless that person waives the right or a court determines the situation is critical enough to override those rights."

"Which to date has never happened," Maddy said. "Good. So for today, we have an individual who was murdered in Boston three days ago. Their will states in the case of any unnatural death, they allow the court to consider a deathbed deposition if it will help determine potential illegal causes of their death."

"How often do you get cases like those?" Tamar asked.

Maddy sighed. "Not as often as we should. There's a lot of disinformation around necromancy spreading, and that means a large contingent of people consider it a violation of their personal autonomy."

"Even in death?"

"Even in death. Next question—what is the first thing we do after we arrive at the hospital morgue?"

"We review the court order and enter it into our case log."

Maddy nodded. "Yes. Because you're an apprentice, we'll enter it in my case log since you operate under my license for now."

"Then we proceed with the deposition in the presence of a lawyer appointed by the court, who is allowed to ask only the preset list of questions."

"Yes. We are legal observers of that part of the deposition. What happens when the questions are done?"

"We retract the partial resurrection. That's the part I'm nervous about."

"It is something different, for sure. But I'll walk you through it when we get there."

The rest of the drive into Boston went smoothly until, just as Maddy predicted, they hit bumper-to-bumper traffic before they even entered the city. Tamar tapped the steering wheel and pretended it wasn't annoying her. The pretense lasted until someone cut her off as their exit came up. She leaned on the horn. "Oh, for crying out loud. Use a blinker!"

She glanced at Maddy. "Sorry."

Maddy let out a soft chuckle. "Well, it's not profanity, so I guess this traffic truly isn't bothering you."

"Profanity isn't really my thing, so I kind of cheated in that promise."

Maddy shifted in her seat, and Tamar felt that focus out of the corner of her eye. "Come to think of it, I don't think I've heard you swear at all."

"Nope." Tamar used a blinker, like any good driver would, and took their exit off the highway. "My grandmother considered it a sign of a weak mind if all you could come up with was swears."

"I doubt she'd approve of my language use, then."

Tamar gave her a quick glance. "I don't think I've heard you swear."

"Much."

"Much," Tamar said. "My grandmother would love you, anyway." Tamar felt the blush creep up her cheeks as she had nothing to back up that declaration but her own feelings for Maddy. Luckily Maddy didn't comment on it as they finished the drive and arrived at Boston Central Hospital.

"I can let you out here and go park in the lot," Tamar said.

Maddy stepped out onto the curb. "Thanks. I'll wait for you inside."

Tamar waited until she was out of view of Maddy before letting out the biggest yawn. So maybe she wasn't as energetic yet as she wanted to be. And maybe a forty-five-minute drive as her first real car excursion wasn't the best idea, but it still felt good to get a bit back to normal.

She parked and joined Maddy in the hospital lobby, where a young woman in a sharp suit paced, talking on her phone until Tamar walked closer.

"Let's get this over with," the woman said. "I'm Leslie Ryatt, and here is my court order approving this deposition."

Maddy let Tamar take the paper from Leslie's outstretched hand. Tamar scowled as she read each line.

"Is there a problem?" Leslie asked.

"My first deposition," Tamar said with a smile. "Just want to be sure I understand the paperwork."

Leslie rolled her eyes. "The morgue is down two levels, if you're quite done?"

Tamar couldn't help taking just that little bit longer to read over the court order, just long enough to sense Leslie the Lawyer was about to explode. "Do you have a pen?" she asked.

Leslie glared at her, but Maddy pulled a pen out of her purse and held out other her hand. "I'm Dr. Maddy Wu. As the licensed necromancer, I'll be signing it. This is my apprentice, Tamar Richler."

"An apprentice? Great. I have a client call in forty-five minutes. Can we speed this along, please?"

To Tamar's surprise, Maddy took a similar long look at the paperwork before signing it. Tamar hid her smile behind a yawn, but she was sure Maddy had taken the extra time just to get under Leslie the Lawyer's skin as well. With paper in hand, Leslie clicked her black high heels to the nearest elevator bank and waited with just as much patience for them to follow.

The morgue had brighter lighting than Tamar expected, but

then the only morgues she'd seen were on television shows. One technician stood waiting for them in an otherwise empty medical room. He took the paperwork from Leslie and stepped into a back room, letting out a cold breeze as he wheeled out a body wrapped in white on an exam table.

"Thank you," Leslie said, somehow conveying how much she didn't mean it with the dry tone of her voice. "We'll come get you when this is over."

With his dismissal, he left the room to them to proceed with their private deposition.

Maddy pulled back the covering to reveal an older man, but Tamar couldn't guess his age. Maddy took out an injector and handed it to her. "We'd normally start with a higher dose, given it's been three days, but we haven't fully tested your blood capabilities, so we'll begin small."

Tamar looked down at the injector that had been filled with her blood over the weekend. "One milliliter?"

"Let's start with half that," Maddy said. "If the dose is too high, we can't let the patient return to the deceased state on his own. That complicates the procedure."

"By all means," Leslie said, "do not complicate this procedure."

Maddy frowned at her but nodded to Tamar to continue. With the injector set at half a milliliter, she pulled down the deceased's collar and injected his cold neck. The goal was to revive enough of the brain to pull out final memories. To her surprise, the man's eyes flickered open, and he let out a rattling breath.

"That shouldn't have worked," Maddy said as she stepped closer to examine the body. She slipped a monitoring band over his head and attached the probes to both temples and the forehead. The lights on each went from red to green, indicating some brain activity.

"Can you tell me your name, sir?"

"George. George Hansellman," he said in a rattling, robotic voice.

Maddy stepped aside. "The patient is ready for you, Ms. Ryatt. Remember he is not alive, but his brain is capable of answering basic questions."

Leslie's cold impatience slipped momentarily as a wave of revulsion seemed to flash across her expression. A moment later, she was back to full lawyer mode and began a series of questions that she recorded on her phone. The entire deposition took less than ten minutes but gave enough evidence, in Tamar's opinion, to arrest the man's next-door neighbor for killing him in a rage.

With the deposition done, Leslie stepped back. "You can end this now."

Mr. Hansellman lay there staring at the lights above him. Little suggested he had any real consciousness, but Tamar couldn't just walk away. She put a hand on his cold wrist. "Thank you for your cooperation. We will get justice for you."

Leslie snorted behind her as she headed for the door, but Tamar ignored the sound. Dead or not quite dead, the man deserved respect for even allowing a procedure like this.

❖

Maddy kept an eye on the monitoring band and didn't like what she was seeing. "His consciousness level is still rising."

"Not a good sign, I guess?" Tamar asked.

"An unusual sign." Maddy didn't say what she was thinking, which was that it was more than unusual. It was unprecedented. "We'll want to test your blood more fully after this to be sure we measure correct dosages."

Mr. Hansellman slowly turned toward her voice, and she swore softly under her breath. "We need to sever the connection between the two of you. This is not normally apprentice-level work, but it's necessary. He's reviving too much from the injection."

"What happens if he revives too much?" Tamar asked.

"There's a reason behind the zombie slang. It's a place we don't want to go to here."

Tamar clenched and unclenched her fists. Maddy reached over to hold her hand. "These things happen. It's not a poor reflection on your skills. Quite the opposite, actually. You're an unusually powerful necromancer."

"Great. How does an unusually powerful necromancer sever the link between herself and her patient before he tries to sit up?"

"You need to extract your life energy from his body. It's… unpleasant."

"Great," Tamar said. "Just freaking great."

Maddy held Tamar's hand a moment longer. "I'd do this for you if I could, but only the necromancer can sever their own link."

Tamar squeezed her hand once, then let it go. "That's okay. It's all part of the package, right? Be a necromancer, raise the dead, and sometimes return the dead to that state."

Maddy nodded and pulled an extractor from her bag. "This will extract a small portion of his bodily fluid. Since he's been in a deep freeze, it will heat his skin to release whatever moisture is left and then draw it into the extractor."

"And then?" Tamar asked.

"And then the unpleasant part. I'll have to inject you with the results."

"Isn't that dangerous? I mean if he died of some contagious disease or something?"

"No, not in that sense. The extractor includes purifying agents to prevent that possibility. But it's an unfortunate experience nonetheless, even without considering the emotional impact."

"You mean the *ew* factor."

Maddy smiled. "Yes, the *ew* factor is definitely part of it. Since this isn't an apprentice-level procedure, I'll do the extraction from Mr. Hansellman and inject you with the results."

She pressed the extractor against his neck, near where Tamar had injected him minutes ago, and turned the extractor on. She felt it hum under her fingers as she held it in place for the requisite two minutes.

When it beeped twice, she removed it and turned to Tamar. "Do you want me to explain what happens next?"

"No. It's just like getting into the cold ocean. Better to just run at it and get the shock over with."

"You'll want to be seated for this."

Tamar looked around. "No chairs. And I'm not hopping on that other gurney. I'll sit on the floor." She lowered herself and sat cross-legged on the floor.

Maddy squatted and sat next to her. "This will sting a bit."

Without waiting, she jabbed Tamar's wrist and emptied the extractor into her flesh. Tamar turned pale and leaned into Maddy, who held her as best she could. She felt Tamar tremble in her arms and held her tighter. She'd done this only once herself, as part of her journeyman training, and remembered how horrible it felt.

"Your body is fighting the effects of Mr. Hansellman. Effectively, you're in a battle between extracting your life energy and him trying to hold on to it."

"That sounds horrible for him," Tamar said through gritted teeth.

Maddy was surprised Tamar could remain empathetic under these circumstances. She settled her weight a bit more comfortably, as this could take some time. She was surprised when Tamar leaned away from her and sat up on her own in less than two minutes.

"It's over," Tamar said.

Maddy frowned. She looked up at the body and saw the headband lights flashing red. "That was fast."

Tamar stood up and offered Maddy a hand to help her up. Maddy needed the help, as her hip joint protested the effort. She pulled her cane from the edge of the gurney and leaned on it to relieve the pain.

"How do you feel?" Maddy asked.

"Besides the *ew* factor? A little tired, surprisingly. Usually after a patient dies, I get that burst of energy."

"This time your body used up that energy by fighting the returning life force in the patient. This is one of the many reasons we try to measure out exact doses. It's not a good experience overall."

Tamar nodded. "How do we test my blood, then? Nice and all to be an uber necromancer, but I'd rather not go through that again."

"Agreed." Maddy started toward the door with Tamar walking to her side. "Kenneth has the best facilities for something like this." She pulled out her phone and sent him a text. To her surprise, he answered immediately.

"He's at our place in Beverly this morning, so will wait for us to get there."

The drive back to Beverly from Boston took less time than the one in. As they pulled up the gravel driveway, she saw Kenneth's gray convertible Volvo in the far parking spot. Once inside the house, all Maddy wanted to do was put her feet up and rest, but she owed Tamar the extra effort to get her capabilities fully tested before another accident like this morning.

"Kenneth?" she called as they entered the foyer.

"Upstairs," he said.

Great, she thought, eyeing the staircase she didn't want to deal with in her tired condition. Tamar must have sensed her reluctance.

"I can go up and talk to him," Tamar said. "You should rest."

"So should you," Maddy said. "And he can come down and talk to us both. He visits once a month to take a sample of Aiden's blood and mine to run through his lab. He can take yours as well down here."

"Meet us in the kitchen," Maddy shouted up the stairs to Kenneth, then made her way into the kitchen and sat at the table.

Tamar poured them both a cup of coffee from the coffeemaker. "It's a little old, but better than nothing." She passed Maddy a cup.

"Thanks," Maddy said, surprised Tamar knew she took hers with just a dash of milk. She closed her eyes as she sipped the warm drink.

Tamar sat on one of the kitchen island stools. "The deposition is different. Like, I didn't feel drained as much as a resurrection and also didn't feel that 'juiced' sensation when the patient died."

"They don't actually resurrect, so technically, they don't die a second time either. But yes, it's less of a drain for sure." Maddy placed her cup on the table as Kenneth swept into the kitchen, looking even more tired than the last time she saw him, but he gave them both a big smile. "You're happy," she said.

"Happy to see my family." He kissed the top of her head. "And you as well, Tamar."

"Her first deposition went well," Maddy said.

"Better than well, from what you texted me. Our Tamar has some necromancer super-powers."

Maddy shook her head but smiled. "Your state lab has more resources than mine. It's important we calibrate her abilities."

"So we don't have another almost-zombie," Tamar said.

"We don't call them zombies," Kenneth said, his smile wavering some. Maddy noted he didn't give his customary wink this time. She was rather glad of that, as it always felt a little false coming from him. It used to be Aiden's habit, not his.

Tamar gave him one raised eyebrow. "What do we call someone animated but no longer capable of being alive? I mean, he was dead for three days. No amount of necromantic blood can bring a body like that fully back to life."

"True. True," he said. "We prefer the term accidentally reanimated."

Zombie, Maddy thought. Maybe if they adopted that term for these cases, people would stop using it as a derogatory term for resurrected people. She wouldn't argue with Kenneth when he was in his must-champion-the-cause mood. He really did look tired.

"Have you been overdoing it?" Maddy asked.

His smile returned. "Not as much as you do, sister." He brushed a hand through his short hair. "Had a resurrection this morning, so yes, I'm showing the fatigue. I'll get over it soon enough."

"I thought when you made necromancer marshal you'd stop doing resurrections," she said.

"Can't capture the highest office for necromancers by being a slacker. I pace myself, but it is the big-ticket resurrections that make the headlines." He put his black briefcase on the counter and pulled out two syringes, already labeled in his scrawling, barely decipherable script.

She waited until Luis came down to roll up her sleeve. Having experienced Kenneth's blood-draw technique in the past, they all agreed it was best if Luis handled them.

Luis took the first set of vials and the syringe from Kenneth. "Ready for your monthly vampire draw?" He smiled as he said it, but Maddy knew he didn't like it when Kenneth took her blood or Aiden's. She couldn't blame him really. She hated it as well.

She barely felt the pinch of the needle, and within moments, she sat with a thumb pressing a gauze pad on her elbow. He replaced her thumb with a bandage and then moved on to take Tamar's blood.

"You'll want to rest for the next couple of days," he said as he finished up and handed Kenneth the full vials.

"I feel fine," Tamar said. "No drawbacks from the deposition."

Luis gave Kenneth an inscrutable look. "Kenneth's tests take a notable drain on his test subjects."

Kenneth laughed and slapped him on the back, a little too hard, in Maddy's opinion. "All for a worthy cause, my friend.

It's only monthly, and it's worth it for the advancements we can make, not just for us, but for all necromancers."

Tamar played with the bandage on her elbow. "What sorts of tests do you run?"

Kenneth's smile faded some. "More detail than you want right now, but we have one of the most sophisticated necromancy labs in the country. Massachusetts is really setting the standard here."

Maddy chuckled. "Practicing your stump speech for that federal appointment?"

"Always," Kenneth said with a grin. "Imagine it, Maddy. We can take what we've done in this state and bring the rest of the country up to our level. Imagine the necromancers we could protect and train with a federal program in place."

She raised her hand. "I'd vote for you for necromancer general!"

"Oh, if only it were an elected office. Still, I have good contacts with this new administration. Maybe it'll happen soon."

❖

Tamar watched Kenneth drive away in his luxury EV. She barely remembered meeting him at the hospital, but he seemed different. Maddy said he looked tired, but Tamar felt it was more than that. He had a grayness to him she'd not noticed the last time. It reminded her of her own patients as they neared the end, but that didn't make sense.

Luis stepped up beside her. "Envious of that toy he drives?"

Tamar shook her head. "Nah. I like my Jeep. Kenneth looks older than his brother."

"You noticed."

"Hard to miss. It's none of my business, but is he ill?"

"Not that I know of, but he won't let me near him."

She turned to him. "Really?"

He shrugged. "Maybe it's a twin thing, since I spend so

much time with Aiden. Maddy never mentions Kenneth being ill. She says he overdoes the resurrections and depositions regularly. I guess that could age a person."

"Yeah. I suppose." She glanced up the stairs where Maddy had headed and pondered what she'd do with herself for the afternoon.

Luis must have noticed her gaze and bumped her shoulder. "I'm guessing Kenneth isn't the Wu who catches your eye, is he?"

"What? No. I mean…"

He laughed. "My father always says, if you have an interest, don't hide it."

"What do you mean?" she asked, not that she didn't understand his meaning, but she needed something to keep her mind off the flush she felt blooming across her cheeks.

Luis turned back to the window. "You know, it's going to be a clear sky tonight. Moon's up right after sunset. Nice night for a beach bonfire."

Tamar glanced quickly up the stairs again. "A bonfire."

He chuckled. "Offer s'mores. She loves them."

Tamar grinned. "Thanks. Might be a great night for a bonfire."

After he left, she hopped into her Jeep and drove to the grocery store for ingredients. When she returned, she still had a couple of hours before sunset so went for a stroll along the beach, looking for the perfect spot. Of course, with a place like this, they already had a series of stones lining a small pit in the sand, with blackened bits of charcoal in it. She tidied it up and even brushed off the big log next to it they could use as a seat. She brought an armload of firewood from the house and then combed the small patch of trees on the edge of the property to find just the right branches to cook the marshmallows on. It all looked perfect, right up to the seals she saw swimming along in the surf in front of her.

Maddy was sitting in the sunroom overlooking the beach when Tamar arrived back at the house. "Tidying up the fire pit?"

Tamar glanced back out the window and realized all her preparations were visible from where Maddy sat. She stuffed her hands into her pockets. "Um, yeah. I was going to start a fire in a bit. Did you want to come out and watch the sunset with me?"

When Maddy didn't answer right away, Tamar added, "We can make s'mores."

Maddy laughed. "Well, I can't resist an offer like that, can I?"

Thank you, Luis! Tamar mentally called over her shoulder as she went to the kitchen. "I'll get all the stuff ready. What do you want to drink?"

Maddy followed her. "We have a fire-pit kettle. I can make hot chocolate."

Maddy pulled out an old picnic basket from the garage, and between the two of them, they filled it up. "I can take this if you can get the kettle and grate for the fire? They're in the back corner of the garage."

Tamar stepped into the garage, staring into the gloom before she spotted the beach supplies propped up against a shelf in the back. She grabbed a colorful woolen blanket as well, to keep them warm as the sun set. By the time she walked back to the fire pit, Maddy had already started a small fire using the branches Tamar had picked for roasting marshmallows.

"I can get more branches for the marshmallows," she said.

Maddy glanced up at her from the log she sat on next to the fire. "No need." She held up an opened package of bamboo sticks.

"Fancy," Tamar said with a grin. She collected a few more kindling branches just in case and sat on the log with Maddy, feeding the flames until the fire took on the larger blocks of wood. She placed the grill over a portion of it, then the kettle. While the water slowly heated, she put her first marshmallow on the end of her bamboo stick.

"Not a bad day, all in all," she said.

"Not a bad day," Maddy said. She pulled out her stick with two marshmallows on it to check it before returning it to the fire. "You did well today. And with Kenneth's tests, we'll have a better idea of how to gauge your injections."

Tamar didn't want to talk shop so switched the subject. "How long have you lived here?"

"Officially, I have an apartment closer to my office, but my parents bought this place when I was about ten."

Tamar did the math in her head. "So four years before the accident?"

"Yes."

Time for another topic switch. "Nice fire pit."

Maddy smiled. "Aiden loved bonfires on the beach, but it was Kenneth who built this the year after the accident. He wasn't much into bonfires until then. It's funny, but he's kind of taken on a lot of Aiden's hobbies since then."

"Maybe it's his way of coping, you know. Must be hard to lose someone, especially a twin."

"Yes. Though they did fight a lot. Kenneth was the stronger necromancer, and I think Aiden was always a bit jealous of that."

Silence settled between them as Tamar struggled for the right thing to say to return a smile to Maddy's beautiful face.

❖

"You like it black?" Maddy asked.

"Huh?"

Maddy pointed to the fire where Tamar's marshmallow was in flames. Tamar pulled it out and blew on it. "I think this is a lost cause."

Maddy laughed. "Not a problem." She pulled one of her marshmallows off her stick and deftly placed it between a graham cracker and a block of chocolate. "For you."

Tamar grinned. "Thanks!" She reached out, but Maddy

pulled the s'more away from her hand and held it closer to Tamar's lips. She watched, mesmerized when Tamar's red lips opened to take a small bite out of her offered gift. She felt those lips brush against the tips of her fingers and couldn't stop the small shiver she felt that had nothing to do with the cool night air.

Tamar's eyes widened as she pulled back. "Son of a beach wagon! That's hot!"

Maddy shook her head. "Son of a beach wagon?"

Tamar grinned. "It's a valid expression. And thanks."

"Maybe you should take hold of the rest of this one yourself and cool it off," Maddy said, offering Tamar the rest of the s'more. Tamar's fingers brushed against Maddy's as she accepted it. Maddy couldn't tell if Tamar's cheeks were flushed from the contact or the heat of the bonfire, but she knew her own were extra warm as the last rays of sunlight disappeared. She busied herself with creating her own s'more and then making the hot chocolate with the water heated in the kettle. She handed Tamar a mug and sipped her own before pushing another pair of marshmallows onto her stick. She wasn't sure what impulse drove her to tease Tamar the way she did, but she couldn't stop the thrill she felt from it.

The first sparkle of stars appeared overhead in the clear, dark sky. Tamar watched them grow brighter overhead until Maddy had to give her a nudge.

"Going two for two?" Maddy asked.

Tamar pulled her stick and flaming marshmallow out of the fire and blew on it. "Okay. Maybe this isn't my strong point."

"How about I roast, and you make them into s'mores?"

"Deal." Tamar pulled out the graham crackers and chocolates and held them on a napkin until Maddy pulled out two more perfectly bronzed marshmallows and handed them to her.

Tamar held one completed s'more to Maddy's lips. "Returning the favor."

Maddy took a small bite out of it, her hand resting on Tamar's. Who knew s'mores could be this interesting?

The wind picked up as the night darkened. Tamar pulled out the blanket she'd brought and held it out. "Getting cold?"

Maddy nodded. "A bit."

Feeling just a little nervous, Maddy moved closer to Tamar on the log. Tamar wrapped the blanket around both their shoulders. It was big enough for them to hold the ends around themselves, with just their sides touching for added warmth. Maddy felt that heat in her core and couldn't think of a thing to say, so she just stared out at the waves curling on the wet sand in front of them.

They sat that way for a time, letting the blaze die down to glowing red embers, until a faint light appeared on the ocean horizon. "Moon's coming up," Tamar said.

Maddy glanced sideways at her. "I'm beginning to think you planned this all out tonight."

Tamar ducked her head. "Well, I had help."

"Luis."

Tamar smiled. "I can't name my source."

Maddy leaned closer. "So considerate of you to protect your source."

Maddy inhaled the scent of Tamar's perfume, a barely discernible, flowery bouquet. After some time like that, she covered a yawn with her hand.

"Time to get back inside?" Tamar asked.

"I suppose. Sorry."

"Don't be. You do a lot, every day. And I could do with an early night as well."

Maddy didn't see any signs that Tamar was tired, but she packed their equipment as Tamar pushed the glowing embers of their fire around to separate them, then kicked sand over the remnants. Together, they walked back to the house, using the glow of the rising moon to light their way.

"Thanks for the s'mores," Maddy said as she flicked on the lamp in the sunroom.

"You're welcome."

Without the cover of darkness, Maddy felt a growing

awkwardness and brushed imaginary sand from her long woolen skirt to keep from trying to hold Tamar's hand. Was something happening between them, or had she just imagined it all?

"What's up for tomorrow?" Tamar asked, stuffing her own hands into her pockets after they put the kettle and basket in the sunroom.

Maddy flicked on a lamp. "I have an appointment in the afternoon to attend a vet surgery at the local rescue hospital. I can't really perform full resurrections anymore, so I do what I can with small animals. It's not such a drain on my energy."

She wanted to extend their time, but a buzz from Tamar's phone pulled her away. Maddy flicked off the lamp and sank onto one of the sunroom chairs to watch the moon rise across the ocean waves. It had been a long time since she'd let herself be attracted to another woman. A smile tugged at her lips. Yes. This felt like maybe the start of something.

CHAPTER NINE

Tamar woke up more energized than she'd been since the car accident. She didn't know why, but she wasn't questioning it. With the September sun shining through her raised shades in the bedroom, she decided it was time to jog along the beach. She pulled on a pair of shorts and the light jacket she'd worn to the deposition and slipped out the back door and down the gravel path to the sand. She left her sneakers and socks by the edge of the fire pit, a smile forming as she remembered the night before.

After a few easy stretches, she walked down to the surf and let the water splash on her bare feet. It felt almost warm compared to the air temperature. She started walking along the shoreline past a family of seals and then moved into a slow jog. She didn't last long before she felt that tug of fatigue that warned her to turn around and start back. She automatically scanned the sand looking for interesting rocks. After skipping a few into the surf, she found one round quartz stone that glowed in the surf line. A sucker for pretty rocks, she picked it up and had unzipped her jacket pocket to put it in when she felt the familiar shape of an injector. She remembered she'd had a spare from the deposition and made a mental note to give it to Maddy after she finished her exercise.

As Tamar crossed the sand by the fire pit, she saw a large gray lump in the sand a few yards ahead. That's when she noticed a pair of younger seals swimming laps in the surf. She rushed up, realizing the gray lump was the momma seal. She hadn't seen what happened, but she could guess. Two pup seals to care for, and one of them must have frolicked too close to the shoreline and was stranded. Momma to the rescue, but Momma didn't make it back into the water.

Tamar dropped beside the seal, ready to shove it into the ocean again. She paused, looking closely. She'd been on enough ocean walks with her dog to realize this seal wasn't going to make it. Squatting, she couldn't keep tears from forming. How long had it been? She glanced between the dead seal and the pups and decided she could do something. She pulled out her injector. If it worked on dogs and cats, it must work for seals as well, right?

She stared at the injector, wondering what the right dose would be. On the one hand, Maddy said her necromancy was strong. On the other hand, this seal had to weigh over a hundred pounds, so easily more than any dog resurrection.

She took a guess and measured out the same amount she'd used on the deposition. Then before she could change her mind and run for help, she jabbed the seal and pushed in her measured amount. She sat back on her heels and waited.

The wait wasn't long. She felt the tug of exhaustion pull at her, and a moment later, she saw the seal's eyes move and its body shuffle. It was still stranded, so Tamar braced herself and shoved.

One-hundred-plus pounds of seal shifted slowly. She shoved again. By the fourth try, the ocean lent her a helping hand and started dragging the seal into the waves. Tamar was knee-deep in the surf when the seal slipped out of her hand and rushed to its waiting family.

Tamar grinned. "Enjoy your swim."

Between the jog and the seal resurrection, she felt exhausted now. As she turned to head back up the beach, a bout of dizziness sent her sprawling into the ocean waves. She sputtered and coughed out salty water, on her hands and knees. Suddenly, the shoreline seemed miles away. Part of her brain recognized the disorientation she felt as an extreme result of another resurrection. She glanced up at the house but didn't even have the energy to call out for help.

She dragged herself into ankle-deep water before the world faded out.

❖

Maddy stifled a yawn as she put on the coffeemaker. Her hip didn't hurt this morning. She wore a long-sleeved black sweater dress and leggings and left her cane upstairs.

Like clockwork, Luis stepped into the kitchen just as the coffeemaker finished its job.

"You have a sixth sense about fresh coffee, you know."

He smiled, pointing to the ceiling. "Hidden cameras."

She poured herself a mug and stepped away from the counter so he could refill his mug. "It's quiet this morning."

"Uh-huh." He grinned as he sipped.

"What's that supposed to mean?" she asked.

"Oh, nothing. Just that a certain necromancer apprentice happened to go out this morning before you woke up."

Maddy heard the tease in his voice but couldn't resist saying, "Her Jeep is still here."

"I'll toss you a bone, sweetie." He patted her on the shoulder as he walked by. "She had shorts on and was headed toward the beach."

Maddy shooed him off, and he left with a laugh. She grabbed her mug and made her way into the sunroom. Not because it had a good view of the beach where Tamar went, but because it would be warm with the morning sun. That's what she told herself, anyway. She paused at the windows. Movement along the beach near the fire pit caught her eye, and she squinted into the bright sunlight to make out what she was seeing.

The mug slipped from her hands, splashing hot coffee across her sweater dress. "Luis!"

She was halfway out the sunroom door when he came in. "What is it?"

"Tamar! She's fallen in the surf!"

He rushed past her. She continued along the gravel drive and down the steps to the sand, cursing her own weakness for not being able to move faster. She watched as Luis stepped into the water and pulled Tamar out.

This isn't happening, she thought. Not again.

Sand dragged at her feet as she pushed herself forward. She'd made it only halfway to Tamar and Luis when he stood up and helped Tamar to her feet. He looped one of her arms over his shoulder and half carried her up the beach.

Maddy grasped Tamar's arm, her jacket sodden from the ocean water. "What happened?"

Tamar just shook her head, the water dripping off her black curls.

"Let's get her inside," Luis said.

Maddy grabbed Tamar's shoes from beside the fire pit, and the three of them made slow progress back to the sunroom. "Put her on the sofa," Maddy said.

"I'm all wet," Tamar mumbled.

"It's seen worse than some salt water." Maddy sat beside her as Luis went to fetch towels. "Let's take some of these wet layers off."

She helped Tamar shrug out of her jacket. To her surprise, Tamar wore only a black T-shirt under the jacket, and it seemed relatively dry. Luis returned and dropped a towel over her shoulders and another across her bare legs.

Maddy felt Tamar shiver under the towels. "Maybe you need a warm bath."

Tamar shook her head. "I don't think I could stay awake for it."

Luis wrapped a third towel around Tamar's dripping hair. "Maddy's right. You need warmth and to get all this salt water off you. I can help."

Tamar looked up at him as if weighing her options, then just nodded.

"I'll start one in the downstairs bathroom," he said.

Maddy held Tamar in her arms, hoping her body heat would help. She was reluctant to let go when Luis returned to help Tamar into the bathroom and made herself busy cleaning up the wet towels. She checked Tamar's jacket pockets before stuffing it in the laundry with the towels, surprised to find an empty necromancy injector in the pocket. Frowning, she put it to the side, assuming it was the one Tamar had used at the deposition. She'd have to talk to Tamar about proper disposal of her injectors.

After twenty minutes, she heard Tamar shuffling out of the bathroom and joined her in what Tamar called the green room. Tamar sat curled up in a blanket on the sofa. Maddy took the side chair. "How are you feeling?"

"Almost as bad as I felt after that accident. Why am I suddenly so exhausted?"

Luis stepped in with a warm mug of hot chocolate for Tamar. "It's Kenneth's so-called experiments."

"Luis," Maddy said. "It's important research."

"Maybe," he said. "But you can't deny the toll it takes on you and Aiden. Maybe some research isn't worth the price."

Tamar glanced between the two of them. "Well, I hope I'm not the subject of his research on a regular basis."

"It's surprising that it hit you this strongly," Maddy said. "I'll call him and find out if he's doing something different."

Tamar rested her head on her propped-up knees. Maddy didn't want to bring up the injector, but she'd probably forget later. "I tossed your jacket into the laundry and removed the used injector. I should have reminded you to dispose of that properly at the morgue."

Tamar looked up. "Oh, I did that. Flushed the remnants of my blood down the bio sink and tossed the injector into the biohazard container."

Maddy frowned. "The injector in your pocket was used."

"There was a stranded seal on the beach. I used it to revive her."

"You didn't." Maddy's temper almost exploded.

"It wasn't that much. And it saved the seal and her cubs."

Maddy stood up. "Do you have any idea what you just risked? I mean besides nearly drowning out there."

"Hey, it was a simple resurrection. I've done it plenty of times before."

"Not when you're still recovering from that car-accident resurrection, and the deposition, and giving blood to Kenneth."

Tamar's temper seemed to flare in reaction to Maddy's. "Well, how was I to know Kenneth's little blood draw would be the equivalent of another full resurrection?"

Maddy squeezed her eyes shut. "So irresponsible."

Tamar stood up. "Well, maybe if the Wu family actually shared their secrets, I'd have known the risks involved."

"Shared secrets? You want to hear our secrets?" Maddy growled.

Luis stepped between them. "Okay, maybe you both need a time-out. How about we start with each of you sitting down before I have to pick one or both of you up." He looked at Tamar. "Again."

"No," Maddy said. "She wants the whole story, so she gets the whole story." Maddy started pacing the small space, the click of her shoes emphasizing everything she was about to say. "As I told you, the accident happened when I was fourteen. Kenneth and Aiden had just turned seventeen and, as usual, were competing with one another. Kenneth was the stronger necromancer. Aiden compensated by being the more political of the two and competitive in every other area. A tropical storm blew in up the coast, and the waves were huge for this area. So Aiden taunted Kenneth into a surf competition. Because I didn't like their competitions and fighting, I stayed in the sunroom."

Tamar folded her arms but didn't interrupt, and Maddy continued. "I didn't see the wave take out Aiden. I wasn't even paying attention. But I did eventually see them both on the beach, one leaning over the other. I couldn't even tell which was which from that distance, since they had matching wetsuits. I ran outside. Oh, yes. I could run back then. I could even surf, but I knew better than to get in the middle of the two of them. By the time I'd reached the shoreline, Aiden was dead. His board had snapped in two. Later, Kenneth told me Aiden had drowned."

She sat back on the chair as the emotions of the event overcame her. "He'd already worked the resurrection, much like you did, I guess, a quick slash of his hand on the broken surfboard. There was a lot of blood on him, but it didn't seem to bring Aiden back. So, like a young fool, I did the same thing, adding my blood to his. I don't know what happened after that since I blacked out."

Tamar came and sat on the floor by her chair, one hand on Maddy's knee. "I'm sorry. You don't have to tell me."

Maddy wiped a tear from her cheek, her anger deflating. "No. I should. There's not much left to tell, really. You see Kenneth recovered, but the dual-blood resurrection didn't work. Aiden healed but remained in a coma. We thought it was temporary, but as you can see, it wasn't. Our parents wanted to let him go peacefully, but Kenneth refused. That's how he ended up as Aiden's legal guardian and probably why our parents now spend most of their time traveling."

Maddy took a deep breath. "The end result for me you can see for yourself. I was too young to have been tested or trained yet, so I learned the hard way that I'm at best a weak resurrector. The extreme energy drain triggered a cascade of medical issues for me. I have chronic fatigue and rheumatoid arthritis that weakens my joints."

"I'm sorry," Tamar said again.

"Nothing to be sorry for. It happened. What's important is that it doesn't happen to you. I know you're a strong resurrector, but no one is sure of what the threshold is between transient necromantic fatigue and permanent damage to the necromancer."

Maddy didn't know when Luis left the room, but he returned with another warm mug for her and set it down on the coffee table.

"If the two of you are okay, I'll head up to check on Aiden." He looked at Maddy. "I'm also going to contact Kenneth and give him a piece of my mind."

"You don't have to," Maddy said. "I can talk to him later."

"And you need rest as well," Luis said. "If Kenneth is running a batch of tests that impact Tamar, we both know what it will do to you and Aiden."

Tamar looked up. "What do you mean?"

Luis headed for the stairs. "I mean his tests always make them both weaker."

Maddy took a sip of the mug without paying attention. "Oh, hot chocolate." Luis knew comfort food was just the right thing for her.

"Are you feeling tired?" Tamar asked, returning to the sofa.

Maddy felt the distance lingering between them but didn't know how to dispel it after her flash of anger. "No. I feel fine. He hasn't tested my blood yet. You should definitely rest today. I'll call him later to find out your test results."

And maybe find out why they hit Tamar so hard. Even with the foolish seal rescue, she shouldn't be in such bad shape.

❖

"Maddy's at the statehouse today," Luis said as Tamar leaned against Aiden's bedroom door.

"You're a mind-reader now?" She took his grin as an invitation and sat in the chair next to Aiden's bed. "He looks better today."

"That he does." Luis finished taking Aiden's blood pressure and wrote it down. "Maddy must have given Kenneth an earful because I don't think he ran any tests after yours on Tuesday, and now it's Thursday."

Thursday, and Tamar had shared only a few words with Maddy since their fight. Their relationship had felt strained since then, with Maddy returning to her apartment on Wednesday. Of course she'd still have lessons with Maddy over the weekend, but that seemed a lifetime away. Tamar just wanted the awkwardness to end.

Luis finished his checks and looked across Aiden's bed at her. "You going to mope here all day or do something about it?"

"Do something?"

Luis looked up at the ceiling and let out a sigh. "Oh, the drama." He turned to her. "She's got a meeting at the statehouse with committee members she can't stand. I'd say, not a bad opportunity to meet her there and offer to drive her home. She'd probably welcome a friendly face."

Tamar stood up as Luis's hint turned into a full-fledged idea. "Thanks. I think I will."

She went back to her room and looked in the closet where she'd put her clothes, trying to pick an outfit that presented a balance between casual didn't-think-about-this-at-all and sexy-but-not-too-obvious. A pair of tight jeans and a black sweater won the battle. Tamar tried to tame her black curls but failed. She headed out the door with a bounce to her step, ignoring the gray clouds overhead. The drive into Boston took less time than usual, but finding a parking spot near the statehouse required an extra twenty minutes.

A light mist fell in Boston Common as Tamar searched for something to take Maddy. She found a great coffeehouse and picked what she hoped would tempt Maddy's appetite. Then she returned to the statehouse, a little damp for not bringing a jacket, but ready to formally apologize for their fight.

She had it all planned, except how to find where the committee meeting was being held. With a bit of extra effort, she discovered the location and headed up the broad stairs to the second level. Her timing worked out for once, as the meeting door opened just as she turned a corner.

With a smile she hoped hid her sudden nervousness, she approached the stream of people leaving, standing to the side as they passed. When Maddy didn't come out of the room, Tamar poked her head inside. The decor had that mix between modern tables with multiple power outlets and an old raised semicircular platform where she guessed the state representatives sat and grilled the committee presenters and each other.

Grilled seemed the right word. Maddy sat on one of those modern tables with her head in her hands. With no one around to prevent her, Tamar slipped into the room.

"Rough meeting?" she asked.

Maddy glanced up at her. "This is a surprise."

Tamar held out the coffeehouse bag. "For you."

A slight smile curved Maddy's lips. "A surprise bearing gifts." She opened the bag. "Muffins!"

Tamar leaned against the table. "Apologetic muffins."

A voice from behind surprised her. "Those are the best kind."

She turned around to face an older Black woman dressed in an off-white suit and tan raincoat. She held out her hand. "I'm Jasmine Bunte."

Tamar took the offered hand. "Tamar Richler."

Jasmine looked down at the bag. "Oh, chocolate-chip muffins. Pure decadence." She smiled at Maddy. "I'd be inclined to accept any apology that came with those muffins."

"Thank you, Representative Bunte," Maddy said.

"And how do you two know each other?" Jasmine asked.

Tamar glanced at Maddy, who gave her a nod. "Maddy is tutoring me to help me get my necromancy license."

"Oh, that's going straight to the top," Jasmine said. "I hope you're worthy of such an esteemed teacher."

"She is," Maddy said, standing up and pulling on her own coat.

"I believe part of your training involves interviewing one of the resurrected," Jasmine said. "Allow me to offer myself for that exercise."

"Um, thanks." As Tamar studied Jasmine, she realized the woman did have that sort of gray look about her. It wasn't something physical, but a feeling Tamar had experienced before. Was it the result of the resurrection? No. It couldn't be that, since Kenneth had a similar look. Maybe the representative was just as overworked as everyone else seemed to be.

"Excellent. Dr. Wu has my private contact information. I look forward to our discussion. Shall we make our way to the congressional elevator?"

Maddy put her muffin back into Tamar's bag. "I think I'll brave the stairs today, but thank you."

Jasmine shrugged. "Talk to you soon, then."

Tamar wasn't sure if she'd addressed that parting comment at her or Maddy. Either way, it felt like Tamar had just stepped into a mess without realizing it.

"Sorry," she said when Jasmine was out of earshot.

"Nothing to apologize for." Maddy watched the door. "Representative Bunte will be an interesting person for your resurrected interview."

Tamar put her hand on Maddy's shoulder. "Seriously, I can find someone else. I didn't realize she was an opponent of yours. I owe you two muffins of apology today."

Maddy smiled for the first time since Jasmine had shown up. "One will be enough. And I owe you an apology as well. I'm sorry I blurted out all my family problems to you the other day. You can't have known how close to home it hit when I saw you out there in the surf."

Taking a risk, Tamar pulled Maddy's free hand into the crook of her arm. "Let's find someplace to eat our apology muffins, then. There's also hot chocolate."

"If I didn't know better, I'd think you were trying to soften my defenses, Miss Richler."

Tamar smiled. "If I didn't know better, I'd think you were about to let me."

Arm in arm, they made their way down the wide stone stairs

to the first level. The sun broke through the clouds as they headed out of the statehouse. All in all, worth the drive, Tamar thought.

❖

Maddy could tell Tamar had something she wanted to share. She finished her delicious muffin and turned to Tamar. "Something on your mind?"

Tamar smirked. "I'm that transparent?"

"That transparent," Maddy said with a smile.

Tamar took a deep breath. "I wanted to explain why I started resurrecting my patients. You know it gives them the chance to say good-bye, but I wanted to explain why that's so important to me. I told you my mom passed when I was young. What I didn't say was my grandmother kept me from her at the end."

Maddy nodded, taking Tamar's hand in hers. "That must have been rough."

"I know she had her reasons, but it's eaten at me that I wasn't with my mom until the end."

"And now you make sure others don't experience that same thing."

Tamar nodded. Maddy wished she could do something to heal the pain still obvious in Tamar's expression, but only time could heal a wound like that. They settled into a companionable silence for a time. Maddy closed her eyes and let the sun warm her cheeks as she sat on a bench that had a picture-perfect view of the statehouse and its golden dome.

"We won't get many more days like this," Tamar said.

Maddy opened her eyes and smiled. "No. Not many. Thank you again for the muffin. I'm sorry I can't head back to Beverly with you. I have an appointment with Kenneth now."

"Oh. I could hang out and wait."

Maddy wanted to prolong her time with Tamar, so it didn't take her long to propose an alternate option. "You could come with me, if you don't mind a somewhat boring discussion."

"Sure." Tamar grinned. "Where's his office?"

"Right here in the statehouse. We'll use the side entrance." Gathering her cane, she took Tamar's offered hand to help her off the bench. Once again, Tamar pulled her hand into the crook over her elbow. Maddy didn't need the level of help Tamar offered, but she didn't intend to complain about the companionship.

Who was she kidding? What she felt was more than companionship, and on a good day like today, she even thought Tamar reciprocated that feeling. The warmth growing in her had nothing to do with the sunlight as they walked past the front of the statehouse.

"Who's she?" Tamar asked, pointing to a bronze statue of a colonial-era woman sitting in a chair right outside the statehouse building.

Maddy stopped in front of it. "Mary Dyer, a Quaker woman executed by the state for practicing her religion."

"Hanged in the Commons," Tamar said, reading from the stone marker in front of the statue. "So much for religious tolerance."

Maddy directed them to the side door, where Tamar continued to look around at everything they passed. "You haven't been to the statehouse much, have you?"

"Not at all," Tamar said. "We lived in Western Mass, so on our school field trips we went to places like Deerfield. I saw the Susan B. Anthony Museum once."

"That's more than I've seen," Maddy said as they walked down the long corridor lined with offices on the left and wide windows on the right.

"We'll have to remedy that for both of us."

Maddy smiled. "And how do you propose we do that?"

"Easy. You obviously have access here, so you can give me the grand tour one of these days. And Rosh Hashanah is a week away." Tamar stopped to face her. "Come with me to my grandmother's farm. It's close enough to make a trip to Deerfield. We can even take in the Bridge of Flowers in Shelburne Falls."

Maddy couldn't help but lean into Tamar. "You make it all sound so appealing."

"It is."

Maddy nodded. "If your grandmother is okay with visitors on short notice."

"Sure, she is. It's a date." Tamar blushed. "I mean…"

Maddy hushed her with a finger to Tamar's lips. "A date."

Maddy's cheeks heated, and she took a deep breath before opening the door to Kenneth's office. He kept his office decor spartan, unlike his old room at home, which still had posters on the walls and Lego models atop his packed bookshelf.

Kenneth sat at his large wood desk and waved them in as he finished a phone call. Maddy took one of the chairs and Tamar the other as he ended it.

"Unexpected treat to see you both," he said. "Did you get to sit in on the committee meeting today, Tamar?"

"No," she said. "I didn't get here until it was over."

"Too bad. I bet it was entertaining."

Maddy snorted. "That's not how I'd describe it. Representative Bunte continues to stonewall most of our ideas."

"Her view of necromancers is stuck in the Dark Ages," he said with his customary wink. "I tried talking to the House majority leader, but there doesn't seem to be any way to have her removed from the committee."

Maddy waved a hand. "Not necessary. She's slowing things down, but she doesn't have enough support to stop it all."

Kenneth turned to Tamar. "Meanwhile, I wanted to apologize personally for the impact my tests had on you the other day. Though you look like you've recovered well."

"Thanks. You look pretty well-rested today as well," Tamar said.

Maddy had to agree. Her brother had a brightness to his expression she hadn't seen in ages. "New exercise routine?" she asked.

"No, more like improving my diet, so I get the nutrients

I need." He leaned forward. "I would like to get more blood samples from you, Tamar. I think we could learn a lot more."

Maddy frowned. "I don't know, Kenneth. Maybe if you send me a summary of the tests you ran, I can help determine why they took such a toll on Tamar. I'd like to be sure it won't happen again. It could be dangerous for her."

He held up his hands. "No need for looking at my tests. The other day was a lab accident that caused too much of her blood to be under test at the same time. I promise this batch will go smoother. I can even call you ahead of time to let you know when the tests will happen. But I don't foresee running them for another month or so."

Maddy wished he wasn't so secretive about his lab setup and tests. They weren't competing, but sometimes he acted as if they were. Maybe they did compete when it came to state and federal grants? Still, they had more to learn from each other, if she could only get him to open up.

"Well, the offer stands," she said, finally.

Tamar glanced at her and then back to Kenneth. "I guess I'm okay with giving more blood, so long as you tell me when the tests run so I can stay in bed or something."

Maddy switched the topic back to the committee, giving Kenneth a full summary and planning next steps. It took another forty-five minutes, and Maddy was exhausted by the end. Politics just dragged on her. She'd much rather spend her time at the lab.

She was also very glad for Tamar's presence. It did calm her to have Tamar drive them back to Beverly as she drifted off to sleep.

CHAPTER TEN

Y ou don't have to interview her, you know," Maddy said as
Tamar finished off her lunchtime smoothie.

"I don't mind," Tamar said. "She seems a nice enough person."

"*Seems* being the relative word."

Tamar picked up the hint that Maddy didn't much like Representative Jasmine Bunte. She assumed it was a political rivalry but didn't want to force Maddy to explain her dislike of the woman. "I need to complete the interview requirement for my necromancy journeyman level, so it seemed like a good opportunity."

Maddy sat silently sipping her tea and pushing her salad around on her plate.

"Not hungry?" Tamar asked.

Maddy grimaced. "Stomach acting up." She pushed the plate away. "I might just have some plain toast instead."

"Want me to get it for you?"

Maddy shook her head. "No, but thanks. You probably need to head out if you're going to be on time. Representative Bunte is a stickler for punctuality."

Tamar grinned and put her and Maddy's dishes into the dishwasher. "Thanks for the hint."

Wednesday traffic was light at one o'clock, so Tamar had

a smooth ride down to Brockton, where Representative Bunte had agreed to meet her at her local office. Tamar found a parking spot two blocks from Bunte's office and made it there with five minutes to spare. It had that aged look that said the internal paneling and furniture had been in place since at least the mid-80s, maybe longer. To her surprise, the only person in the small place was Bunte herself.

"Representative, thanks for offering to be my interview candidate," Tamar said, holding out her hand.

"Please, call me Jasmine." She shook Tamar's hand and pointed to an old sofa that lined one wall. "Have a seat. Do you want anything to drink?"

"No, thanks." Tamar sat and pulled out her laptop. "Do you mind if I type your answers in directly as we go along? Makes the paperwork easier."

"No problem." Jasmine took a seat next to her, holding a warm mug. "I assume you have a fixed set of questions to ask?"

Tamar smirked. "Yeah, sort of."

"This will be interesting," Jasmine said. "And might inform me on how best to steer this questionnaire in the coming necromancy legislative updates."

"The stuff you're working on with Maddy?"

Jasmine laughed. "Well, I'm not sure she'd agree that we're working together on it. We have somewhat differing views on where necromancy should go in this state."

Tamar felt like she'd stepped on a landmine there and glanced down at her questionnaire on her laptop to avoid following up on that comment. "Okay. First question seems kind of invasive. Sorry about this. The question asks, How did you decide whether to allow a necromancy resurrection in your medical directives?"

"Easy enough," Jasmine said. "At the time, legalized necromancy in Massachusetts was a new thing. I think most of us at that point signed up to support both the legislation and the benefits we saw in having another medical intervention for a critical patient." She smiled. "At the time, I never thought I'd need it. I was twenty-six years old and the newly elected representative from Brockton."

Tamar glanced up from her typing. "Sounds like you've had a change of heart?"

"Perceptive of you. I'm sure there's a question coming about the resurrection experience itself?"

Tamar looked down. "Yes. The next question."

Jasmine leaned back and put her mug on a side table. "Officially, I died two years after signing my resurrection directive. A car accident."

Tamar's thoughts flashed to the person she'd resurrected a few weeks earlier. "That's a common scenario, I hear."

"Yes. That and drug overdoses are the top two resurrection scenarios in this state. Anyway, I won't bore you with too many details. Mainly, I woke up in the hospital. I wouldn't have known I'd died if the hospital's staff necromancer, Kenneth Wu, hadn't been in my room shortly afterward to explain what had happened. Part of my proposal differences with Dr. Maddy Wu is her insistence that we continue to have a licensed necromancer explain the resurrection to a resurrected patient. Frankly, I think it would all go smoother if a doctor or nurse handled that part."

Tamar nodded as she typed. "I can see that. None of my license training deals with people skills, so to speak."

"Perhaps you can share that opinion with your mentor, then?" Jasmine smiled. "Something tells me she might listen more to you than to me."

Tamar's cheeks warmed. "Um. Yeah. The next question…"

Jasmine held up a hand. "Before we move on. Something else that hasn't been made clear to people signing up for a resurrection—the aftereffects of it all. How old would you guess I am, Tamar? Don't be shy. I can take the truth. Lord knows I look at it every morning in the mirror."

Another landmine in front of her, but Tamar had no way

to avoid an answer. "I'm not good at picking ages. I guess late forties?"

Jasmine tapped her arm. "Now you are being too polite. Most impartial estimates put me in my fifties. As do my medical records. My actual age is thirty-five."

Tamar couldn't school her expression fast enough.

Jasmine gave her a nod. "Yes. You see, even in your necromancy training courses, they aren't covering the long-term effects of resurrection. I went from being a twenty-eight-year-old woman to walking around in the body of someone at least a decade older, and that clinical age gap is only growing. Do you know the average life expectancy of a resurrected?"

Tamar shook her head.

"Fifty-nine."

"That's..."

"That's a well-known fact in necromancy research that certain parties refuse to put into the literature the average person receives when they're asked to accept or decline resurrection in their medical records. And no, it's not Dr. Wu who is holding out against this disclosure. That comes from her brother Kenneth, our state necromancer marshal. His department owns the legal framework for what people sign up for, as well as the details on the state government website."

"Sorry," Tamar said. "That doesn't seem right."

"Glad you agree, dear. Don't get me wrong. I am grateful Kenneth gave me a part of himself to bring me back to life. But we need to go further here, at the state level at least. If I am to die before I reach sixty, then maybe we resurrected should be eligible to tap in early to our Social Security benefits, or disability, and so on."

Tamar glanced at Jasmine and noticed the skull pin she wore. "Zombie rights?"

Jasmine smiled. "Does it surprise you that we coopted the term some people use against us? It takes their own prejudice and directs it toward them. We aren't a big political faction, but we do have allies that join us in letter-writing campaigns and political pressure."

Tamar kept to the predefined questions for a time, not sure how to process what Jasmine was telling her, but the final question was an open-ended one. "Anything else you want to tell me as a potential necromancer?"

Jasmine leaned forward and put a hand on her arm. "First and foremost, thank you. Another item not publicized well is the impact resurrections can have on the necromancer. Dr. Wu has suffered for years after her attempt with her brother. Part of what I want to see implemented is better protections for minors. It's one of the items she and I agree on. I thought I had her support on a registration requirement as well, but she seems to have changed her view on that one."

"A registry of necromancers starting in middle school? I agree with her on that." And had maybe influenced Maddy's evolving view. Tamar could just hear her grandmother's voice in her head warning of the end results when anyone is categorized by something they have no control over. "That sort of thing never ends well."

Jasmine nodded. "Yes. I can see that from your perspective, and perhaps there is room for compromise here, but the goal is important. We need to prevent our young people from hurting themselves and potentially others by using their innate talent without training."

"That seems fair," Tamar said.

"I just wish our necromancer marshal shared your willingness to compromise. I know Dr. Wu might be convinced, but her brother is in a different world than the rest of us sometimes. His ambition controls his actions, and his actions, unfortunately, dramatically impact the state's legislation."

Tamar closed her laptop since they were done with the interview questions. "I don't know Kenneth well. I mean, I've seen him from time to time." She didn't much like talking about him because she still felt awkward about him hiding her unlicensed resurrection for her. She didn't like owing a relative stranger for something that important.

"Lucky you. My advice, stick with Dr. Wu. We may be political opposites, but I respect her opinions and her willingness to hear me out on issues. And her research is more open than her brother's. He has yet to release summaries of his ongoing projects, though the state budget has been funding them for years."

"Yeah. Maddy can't seem to get my test results from him either."

Jasmine raised an eyebrow. "He's running tests on you?"

Tamar wished she'd kept her mouth shut. How to backtrack that one? "Well, it's part of the licensing, I guess. He needs to verify the strength in my blood for resurrections so I don't over, um, resurrect what should be a deathbed deposition."

"Interesting." Jasmine stood up. "Well, this has been an educational opportunity for the both of us. I'm sure we'll have the chance to talk again, soon."

That comment came across more ominous than Jasmine might have intended. Tamar gathered her belongings to hide her discomfort. "Thanks again."

She was glad to be out of that office and heading home. Well, to Maddy's home. After a few weeks, she didn't know how much longer she'd be staying there, and the thought of leaving bothered her more than she'd imagined it would. Still, she had this weekend to share with Maddy at her grandmother's house for Rosh Hashanah.

❖

Maddy sat at the kitchen table watching Tamar at work. She had half the kitchen counter covered in flour as she kneaded the dough she'd made from scratch. Maddy was tempted to tell her she had a splash of flour across her pale cheek as well, but it was too cute to risk Tamar wanting to wipe it clean. "So why the four strands of dough?"

Tamar glanced at her over her shoulder, showing off that flour and her deep-red lips. "It's to braid it. It's a challah loaf, but instead of the standard braid, I'll make it round, and that needs four strands. Do you want to come help?"

Maddy approached the mess formerly known as a counter-top. She cleaned and dried her hands, then applied some flour to keep them from sticking to the dough. "How can I help?"

"Easy. It's a weaving pattern. Like braiding hair, almost."

Maddy smiled. "I can't picture you braiding another girl's hair."

"Oh you'd be surprised what a teen lesbian will do to impress a girl."

"Like braiding a fancy Jewish loaf of bread?"

Tamar blushed. "Maybe. Here, you take these two, and I'll manage the others. We'll take turns on the weave."

The pattern was simple, yet heat rose in Maddy's cheeks as they worked so close her shoulders brushed Tamar's on every over-and-under of the weave. She felt disappointed when it was done, yet a bit proud. "That does look round and braided."

"Never doubt my culinary skills," Tamar said as she set the loaf back under a towel to rise one more time.

"Oh, I've seen your culinary skills."

"Yeah. Maybe they aren't the greatest, but I can do a few things well. My grandmother taught this to me when I was eleven, and I've been making the Rosh Hashanah challah bread ever since."

Maddy cleaned her hands and helped Tamar put the kitchen back into some type of order. "You're sure your grandmother doesn't mind the company?"

"Oh, not at all. Samantha and her boyfriend will be there as well." Tamar's blush deepened. "I mean, Nanna is fine with me bringing a friend. She loves company out there."

Maddy smirked and took her seat again. Making Tamar blush could just become her favorite pastime. "I suppose I should pack. Anything in particular I should take?"

"Pajamas," Tamar said with a wink that caused Maddy's cheeks to heat again. Teasing could go both ways. "And a warm jacket. Nanna likes to use the stream out back as part of her religious rituals."

"You know I'm not religious at all. Is that okay?"

"Oh, sure. You don't have to participate in that part if you don't want to. It's kind of nice, though. We take bits of this bread out to the stream. Nanna says a prayer in Hebrew, and then we toss the pieces into the stream, letting it carry away last year's sins. Though I prefer to think of them as regrets and mistakes. It's a nice way to clean house, so to speak, before Yom Kippur."

Maddy had lived with a Jewish roommate in college, so she'd heard some of this before, but she still felt a little awkward intruding on a family gathering. "Okay. I can pack a coat. And my sins."

Tamar smiled. "Good thing about sins, they don't take up room in the luggage."

Maddy made her way out of the kitchen with one final tease. "Oh, you underestimate my sins."

Leaving Tamar with her cheeks a lovely rosy color, Maddy went upstairs to pack for an overnight stay in Western Massachusetts. The first thing she packed was the woolen dress Tamar had complimented her on a week before. She added a silky nightgown, not that she anticipated anything, but it felt good to include something pretty. She took out her traveling pill case and handled the task of packing the day and a half's worth of medications she needed. And she took her cane as well.

Maddy popped her head into Aiden's room to say good-bye to him. Luis sat there reading to him from one of his sci-fi books he'd loved as a teen. Sometimes she wondered if he was sick of hearing the same old story over again, but then who knew what he heard?

"On your way?" Luis asked.

"Yes. Can you help me get my luggage down the stairs?"

"No problem." He stood up. "Remember to pack something sexy?"

"Oh my God."

Luis tapped her arm on the way by. "You never know."

Maddy knew, though. She wasn't the type to sleep with someone, especially someone she hadn't even kissed yet. What was he thinking? That thought ran circles around in her mind as they put everything into Tamar's Jeep. What did Maddy expect out of this trip, and why had she agreed to it?

❖

Maddy sat in silence as Tamar started the car and headed to the highway.

"Something on your mind?" Tamar asked.

Maddy sat up straighter. "No, not really."

Tamar shot her a quick glance. "I realize we haven't known each other long, but even I can tell when you're stewing on something, Dr. Wu."

Maddy laughed. "It's Dr. Wu now, is it? Fine. Yes, I am wondering about what to expect this weekend."

"Oh, easy enough. Nanna will shower you with invasive questions, attempt to convince you that gefilte fish is tasty, and in general get you to eat far more than you intended."

"That's supposed to make me feel better?"

"Okay. Maybe not," Tamar said with a smile. "Avoid the gefilte fish, by the way. It really isn't very nice. Nanna loves it, though. As for the questions, they won't necessarily be personal, but she is a retired professor of philosophy, so we can pretty much guarantee some kind of deep conversation that's hard to follow if you don't live in Nanna's brain."

Maddy visibly relaxed. "Okay. I think I can handle that."

Tamar tried to keep the conversation light, but an

uncomfortable awkwardness was taking over. Her attraction to Maddy had only grown, and they'd be together overnight at her grandmother's house. She'd invited Maddy on the spur of the moment, not thinking Maddy would accept. Now she felt both the anticipation of what might happen and the fear of misjudging the whole thing and making a fool of herself.

The drive along Route 2 was slightly longer, but the winding, tree-lined road already had fall colors on display in some places. It would be great to see her dog, Kalev, again after so many weeks. "Hey. You haven't met my dog yet, have you?"

"No, but you've shown me pictures. A beautiful black Lab mix, right?"

"Yes. I hope you like dogs."

"Yes. I like all animals. I introduced you to my pet tortoise already."

"Yes. A tortoise named Donatello," Tamar said with a laugh.

"No pet-mocking," she said and grinned. "It was Kenneth's before the accident. After, he just didn't seem interested in Thor, so I took him."

"Thor? He named his tortoise Thor?"

Maddy laughed. "Yes. It's an odd name, but Kenneth named him when he was in his Marvel comics phase. So, yes. Thor."

"God of Thunder. Carries his own shell."

Maddy slapped her lightly on the arm. "I renamed it. And what's your dog's name, then?" Maddy asked.

"Kalev. You'll love him. He's super friendly."

"Kalev?"

Tamar winced. "Okay, not the most creative name. It's Hebrew for dog."

"Do you speak Hebrew?"

"Not really," Tamar said. "Nanna does. I can barely make it through Friday prayers with her. I'm not really religious, but things like Rosh Hashanah, Yom Kippur, and Hanukkah are family times."

Maddy stared out the window. "Our parents raised us Methodist, but Kenneth and I don't really do much with it anymore."

"Not even Christmas? I mean as a Jew, I confess to a certain level of jealousy over that one."

Maddy turned to her. "Well, maybe we can celebrate Christmas this year, just to return the favor. You can come over for a nice roast dinner."

Tamar couldn't stop the wide grin on her face. Maddy assumed they'd be together through Christmas. That glow lasted all the rest of the way to Peterborough. She took the final turn onto the gravel drive that led past a pair of overgrown horse pastures until the house and barn came into view. "We're here."

❖

Maddy stepped out of the Jeep and took in her surroundings. A two-story red clapboard house stood in front of her, and she was glad she'd brought her cane for those inevitable stairs. The front of the house was edged with burnt orange, as well as red hardy mums. A smattering of similarly colored leaves floated down from the surrounding maple trees.

Two other cars sat parked in front of the double doors to the big red barn adjacent to the house. "Who else is here?" Maddy asked.

"That's Nanna's old Prius," Tamar said as she pulled luggage out of the back of the Jeep. "I don't recognize the silver sedan. I'm guessing that's Samantha's new car."

"She's your cousin, right?"

"Yep." Tamar's luggage consisted of an overstuffed backpack. She slipped her arms into the straps as Maddy reached for the handle of her own bag. Tamar gently pushed her hand away. "I can drag it."

Maddy could have insisted that she was able to carry her

own luggage, but that would have been a lie, given she'd struggle just climbing the handful of wooden steps that led up to the wide wraparound porch. She pulled her cane out of the back of the Jeep. "Thank you."

The front door opened just as they started up the steps. A short, older woman stepped out, her gray hair wrapped in a green scarf and a smile on her face. "Tamar!" She held her arms wide until Tamar stepped into the embrace.

"Hi, Nanna." Tamar separated herself and turned back to Maddy. "This is my friend, Maddy."

"Welcome, Maddy. I'm Judith." She wrapped Maddy up in a quick hug. "Glad you could join us this weekend."

They stepped inside to be met by the glare of a tall, bleached-blond woman dressed immaculately. This other woman eyed Maddy, who somehow felt she'd come up lacking in some way. Maybe because she didn't have the perfect thin figure?

The woman stepped closer. "So this is the necromancer?"

Maddy squared her shoulders. That was the reason for the glare. Well, she'd faced prejudice before for multiple reasons. "I'm Dr. Wu, yes." And yes, she was not above slinging her professional accomplishments about in the face of anyone willing to judge her without even knowing her.

"Samantha Ross." Judith slapped the woman with the dish towel in her hand. "Your mother raised you better." Judith turned to Maddy. "Excuse my other granddaughter. She was raised by wolves."

"Sorry, Nanna." Samantha said the words, but her cold eyes told another story.

"Knock it off, Samantha," Tamar said, dropping the luggage on the wooden floor with a thump, close enough to make Samantha back up a step. Tamar took Maddy's hand. "Samantha likes to think she's my protector, but mostly she's just an old nag in a young body."

Samantha let out a heavy sigh. "Fine. Sorry, Dr. Wu. I

shouldn't take out my frustration on you. Tamar's the one who's done the about-face and jumped into this necromancy thing with both feet and no common sense."

Tamar laughed. "See? She even talks like she's eighty."

Maddy relaxed some. "No offense taken." She held out her hand. "Call me Maddy."

Samantha gave her a quick shake, then picked up Tamar's backpack. "I'll help you get these up the stairs."

Tamar handed her one of the suitcases instead. "Where's your boyfriend?"

Maddy heard Samantha explain his absence as the pair walked away toward the staircase. She had the feeling Samantha would be grilling Tamar during that trip, but she resisted the urge to follow them up. Whatever bias the woman had, Tamar would have to deal with it on her own now that she was getting her necromancy license.

"Come on in and have a seat. It's a long drive from the coast," Judith said. She led them past the wide staircase that Tamar and Samantha had disappeared up and into the main part of the house. The open floor plan let in sunlight from windows on the front and side of the house, brightening the cozy living room. Maddy sat on a gray sofa covered in crocheted blankets. Judith stepped out of the room for a moment and returned with a large glass of water with a lemon slice.

"I'm sure you didn't drink enough on the drive," Judith said, handing her the glass. It was a statement, not a question, and Maddy smiled into her glass.

Judith sank into a rocking chair next to the unlit fireplace. "While those two are upstairs airing out their differences, let's air out ours as well."

Maddy's spine went rigid again. "Which differences would those be?" And why had Tamar left her here to be grilled by yet another of her relatives?

Judith smiled warmly. "We're a blunt family. Something

you'll get used to, I'm sure. But I feel it's best to clear the air quickly and get it over with."

"Like pulling off a Band-Aid," Maddy said.

"Right. No sense in little tugs. Just rip it off. I raised Tamar after her mother died, and I raised her to not become a necromancer. Now, I don't want to get your dander up any more than Samantha already has. It was and always will be Tamar's choice what she does with her abilities. But you both need to accept where necromancy is going in this country. Prejudice doesn't just disappear because something's been legalized."

Maddy nodded. "Agreed. And I think you'll also agree that we can't limit our lives based on other people's prejudices."

Judith's smile widened. "I'm going to like debates with you. Yes, agreed. Live your true selves. But live those selves with the awareness of what not only can but will go wrong. Necromancy is still new to the common public, and newness means there will be backlash. Please, protect yourselves against that happening."

Tamar stepped into the room. "So what are you two talking about?"

"Necromancy," Judith said.

Tamar blanched. "Nanna."

Maddy patted the sofa next to her. "Come sit. No first blood has been drawn here."

"So far," Tamar muttered as she sat next to Maddy, their legs just touching.

Samantha entered the room with a plate of apples and honey and crackers that she placed on the central coffee table. "What have I missed?"

"Just in time to change the topic," Tamar said.

"From what to what?" Samantha asked as she dipped an apple slice in some honey.

"From necromancy to something less controversial," Tamar said.

"No," Maddy said, squeezing Tamar's hand before letting go. "If your family has questions or worries, let's hear them out."

Judith nodded. "Yes. I am going to like having you here, Maddy."

"You like anyone willing to argue with you," Samantha said.

"I like anyone willing to debate," Judith replied. "So let's debate, and then we can eat."

Samantha wiped her fingers on a yellow cloth napkin. "Okay. Debate. Point. Necromancy will get Tamar in trouble."

"Counterpoint," Tamar said. "Necromancy has already gotten me in trouble, remember? Maddy and her brother got me out of it."

Maddy wasn't surprised that Tamar had told her family the truth about her situation. "Point. Tamar's necromantic skills are exceptional and can improve the lives of many people. Should she not use those skills for the betterment of others?"

"Point well made," Judith said. "Counterpoint. Isn't Tamar already dedicating her life to others as a hospice nurse?"

"Point," Tamar said. "Tamar is right here and sick of being talked about like she doesn't get to make her own life choices."

Judith smiled. "Okay, Tamar. Make your case."

She leaned forward. "Point. I don't have to make any case. My own life choices, remember? Point. Maddy has done everything she can to help me learn and control what I've been using all along anyway. Point. I can't and won't live my life in the shadow of someone else's biases. Every one of us here is subject to potential social backlash. Maddy is Chinese American. We're Jewish. Maddy and I are queer. Samantha could be the target of a stalker just based on her good looks."

Thanks," Samantha said. "For the compliment and the worry."

As they went into the kitchen, Maddy was surprised and grateful that Tamar's response had ended that particular debate. While it had been an invigorating discussion, she'd hoped for a more peaceful weekend.

Tamar pulled her challah bun out of the bread bag and put it on the cutting board. "I think it came out well, don't you?"

Maddy glanced over her shoulder. "Perfect golden crust."

Samantha took a small ceramic bowl from the cupboard. "Put the pieces in this."

"How many pieces do we need?" Tamar asked.

"How many sins you got?" Samantha asked with a raised eyebrow.

"Less than you." Tamar pulled one section of braid out with her hands and broke it into multiple pieces in Samantha's bowl. "That should be enough, even for you."

Samantha stuck out her tongue and marched out the back door, where Nanna waited. Maddy slipped her hand into Tamar's. "Do we say our regrets and sins out loud?"

Tamar squeezed her hand. "No. It's all kept inside you. And you don't have to do it if you don't want."

"No. I want to. I have some regrets I wouldn't mind casting away."

Tamar wiggled her dark eyebrows. "Deep, dark regrets?"

"None-of-your-business regrets!"

They followed Nanna and Samantha down a dirt path behind the house and through the patch of old oak and maple that spread out beyond. The path cut to the left and opened up under a broad willow, whose branches reached down to just above the water level of the stream that wound around it. A boulder split the stream in two for a short span before it joined again to continue flowing out of view around a bend.

Nanna took the bowl of bread bits and spoke the Hebrew prayer Tamar remembered from her childhood. Then Judith took a few bits of bread and handed the bowl to Maddy as the next oldest in the group.

"Just take what you want, and toss them in one at a time," Tamar whispered.

Maddy took a few and handed the bowl to Samantha.

Tamar had the last few bread bits as the youngest in their group. She stepped to the edge of the stream, where bread already floated by her, and thought about the year just past. She tossed in one piece of bread for the argument she'd had a week before with Maddy. Another piece of bread covered her guilt over using her necromancy without training. She didn't regret how or why she'd done it, though.

The final bit of bread for her represented the things she'd done that she couldn't remember anymore but were sure to have hurt other people's feelings and whatnot.

With that over, they made their way back to the house and the delicious meal Nanna had made for them. She even enjoyed a glass of wine from the two bottles Samantha had brought. With the sun set and the sky completely dark, she leaned over to Maddy next to her on the sofa. "Have you seen the stars at night?"

Maddy turned to her. "Well, I haven't looked up recently, but I'm guessing they're still there."

"Funny," Tamar said with a grin. "You're in for a treat." She stood up and held out her hand.

Maddy took the offered help and stood up. "I guess we're going outside?"

"You guessed right!"

Tamar handed Maddy her light coat and pulled on a jacket as well. She offered Maddy her arm as they walked down the back stairs and along the dirt path and into the woods.

"Hard to see stars in a pine forest," Maddy said.

"Just wait. Not far from here." Tamar knew the perfect spot for stargazing. She'd been walking this path at night for years, and with Rosh Hashanah signaling a new moon, the stars had no competition. They walked for five minutes, guided by the beam of a flashlight, before Tamar paused. "You need to close your eyes now."

Maddy raised an eyebrow. "Seriously?"

"Seriously."

Maddy complied. "If I trip over a root, I'm blaming you."

Tamar grinned. "I can accept that responsibility." She used

the excuse to wrap an arm around Maddy's waist as she led her along the final section of the path. The trees cleared to a broad meadow, and she guided Maddy to the center. "Okay. You can open your eyes now."

Maddy looked around and then up. "Oh my God. This is amazing."

The wide band of the Milky Way stretched across the sky, connecting treetop to treetop across the clearing.

"I've never seen this many stars," Maddy said, walking a small circle around Tamar as she kept her eyes on the sky.

"You need to get out of the city more," Tamar said.

"It's beautiful."

Tamar stopped Maddy's slow circle. Her pulse raced as she put both arms around Maddy's waist. "Beautiful sky for a beautiful woman."

Maddy turned to her. "I'm not sure if I should be flattered or groan at that."

Tamar grinned. "A little of both, maybe." She brushed a strand of hair off Maddy's cheek and tucked it back behind her ear. Maddy leaned closer. Tamar followed, focusing on Maddy's lips, shutting her eyes when those lips met hers. The kiss started as a gentle brush. Maddy wrapped her arms around Tamar as the kiss deepened until they both had to stop to catch their breath.

Maddy rested her forehead against Tamar's. "Thank you for inviting me up here."

"Thank you for saying yes."

The erratic beam of a flashlight shone along the path they'd walked down. Tamar frowned. "Well, so much for this quiet moment."

Maddy took a step back but kept an arm around Tamar's waist as Samantha appeared at the edge of the clearing.

"Thought I'd find you here," Samantha said. She wore her long coat and a pair of heels that couldn't be easy to walk in along that dirt path.

"You've found us," Tamar said. "Now how about leaving us?"

Samantha flashed the light at both of them, and Tamar had to turn her head. "You're ruining our night vision."

Samantha let the beam fall to their feet. "Yes. Well, it's not like I wanted to stomp out here tonight. This has probably ruined my heels. But there's a call for Maddy at the house."

Maddy padded her pockets. "I left my phone up there."

"And your brother is not a patient man, I take it," Samantha said. "He called the house phone."

Tamar wondered how he'd gotten the number and then recalled the information she'd had to fill out for him and Maddy when she signed up for necromancy lessons. "Did he say why he called?"

"Do I look like an answering service?" Samantha said as she turned. "I delivered the message. Now I'm getting back to the house to see if I can keep these shoes from ending up a complete wreck."

Tamar's eyes adjusted again to the dark, but Maddy pulled away. "I should go see what he wants."

With a sigh, Tamar flicked on her own flashlight and led them back to the house, wishing unpleasant thoughts on Kenneth and Samantha both for interrupting their first kiss.

CHAPTER ELEVEN

Maddy dialed Kenneth back on her phone as soon as they returned to the house. "What's so urgent that it couldn't wait until tomorrow?" she asked in lieu of saying hello.

"Good evening to you too, Maddy. I wanted to give you a heads-up that your lab will be under a state audit starting Monday."

Maddy gripped the phone harder. "What? Why now? You know I have important projects ongoing."

Tamar sat beside her at the kitchen table with a growing frown. Maddy held Tamar's hand, which acted as both a comfort to her and a way to let Tamar know all was okay, even if it wasn't. Kenneth had never put her lab under close scrutiny before. They had a casual agreement that since they effectively competed for the same federal grants, they would keep their work separate from one another. And frankly, he had far more resources than she did, so her work should have no impact at the state level.

"Maddy, I'm sorry, but I have reports on a project you're running, off the books so to speak."

Maddy grew stiff. She knew what project he was talking about. But she didn't know how he'd found out about it. "I have a discretionary budget for experimental projects. It's part of my contract."

She could hear the strain in his voice as he tried to smooth this situation. "Maddy, you're testing Aiden's blood."

And there was the crux of the matter. "I'm only running comparison tests. Nothing I'm doing can harm him in any way."

"That will be up to the audit to determine. I'm sorry, sister, but there are laws."

Laws he regularly flouted when he wanted to, Tamar being the most recent example. She tried her final card. "You have medical power of attorney for Aiden. You can authorize the tests."

"We can discuss that option later. I need to head out, but I thought you should know before the audit starts. I shouldn't be telling you about even that much, but you're my sister. It would be best if you destroyed any of Aiden's blood samples before the audit starts."

So he was giving her a chance to clean up and sweep her research under the carpet. She didn't know whether to thank him or scream at him for triggering an audit in the first place. She went with the neutral "Good-bye."

Tamar squeezed her hand. "Doesn't seem like it was good news."

"No. It's not." She turned to Tamar. "I'm sorry. I need to get to my lab tonight. I haven't unpacked yet, so I can just call an Uber. Can you apologize to your grandmother for me?"

"Apologize for?" Judith stepped into the kitchen.

Maddy took a deep breath. She'd need to explain it to Tamar anyway. "My research lab is being audited Monday. Since I have critical projects in the works, I need to head there now and see what I can finalize before the state steps in."

Judith nodded. "Regulatory restrictions."

More like regulatory overreach, Maddy thought.

"I can drive you," Tamar said.

"No. That's not right. This is your holiday."

"Who is qualified to judge what is right and what is wrong?" Judith sat at the big farm table, cleaned now from their dinner. "Who is to say which is the better way to acknowledge the holiness of a day? Perhaps it is holier to help a friend in need than to linger after a meal enjoyed with family and friends?"

Maddy didn't know how to take that statement, but Tamar grinned at her. "This is life with a philosopher. I'll bring our bags back down, and we can head to your lab."

The drive back to Beverly was quiet. Maddy dozed off from the steady rhythm of the car on the Pike now instead of the back roads Tamar had taken to Peterborough. She woke up again as they left the highway behind. "We're in Beverly already?"

"Yep. Are you sure you're up for this tonight? You seem tired."

She felt tired, always tired. "I'll be fine. You can just drop me off. I may be there most of the night."

"And leave you to try to find an Uber after midnight? I'll be fine. I can bug you with a thousand questions while you work. Sounds fun, right?"

Maddy shook her head and smiled. "You and I define fun a different way."

The lab building was deserted at this hour on a Friday night. While the front of the building had bright lights, the inside had little but the glow of security lights. As they walked in, the motion-sensitive lights flicked on. Maddy led them to the elevator and up to her lab.

"Anything I can help with?" Tamar asked.

"Actually, yes." Maddy sat at her lab desk and logged into the network. She shuffled in her desk drawer and pulled out one of her memory sticks. "Are you able to wipe this stick clean and then download some files for me?"

"Sure."

She left Tamar there with a list of directories to download onto the memory stick and went to scan the status of ongoing lab tests from another computer on one of the lab benches. She'd had enough time during the drive to decide which reports were most important, and the one that triggered the audit was at the top of her list. First, though, she checked each machine to see when current tests would finish. Luck was on her side, as two of them would resolve in the next hour, and she could download the reports. The last one that involved Aiden's blood wouldn't finish. "Shit."

Tamar pulled a lab stool up next to her and handed her the memory stick. "Problems?"

"Yes." Maddy ran a hand through her hair and stared at the dark window facing them. "This is the test that got Kenneth's attention." She turned back to Tamar. "Strictly speaking, it's not an officially funded research project."

Tamar's eyes widened. "You, skirting the rules? Must be something special."

Maddy sighed. "I'd hoped it would be. I'll have to stop the test early and just see what results I might get."

"What's it testing?"

"Two things, really. First, can we determine from bloodwork whether a necromancer is a resurrector or limited to depositions? Right now, we can tell only by experimenting on cadavers. It would be vastly more efficient to prove this difference with bloodwork."

"That doesn't sound bad. Why would Kenneth want to stop that?"

"Besides it not being funded?" Maddy asked. "Necromancers protect their blood. It's nearly impossible to get a licensed necromancer to agree to additional blood tests. Until a necromancer is trained and licensed, we don't know if they can or cannot do resurrections."

"So your pool of licensed necromancers is small."

Maddy nodded. "Practically nonexistent. I've been running the tests based on my blood and Aiden's. I can resurrect, in limited scenarios. The accident happened before Aiden was licensed, but we knew he didn't have nearly the abilities Kenneth had. That gave me two data points to run the tests against."

"So why is Kenneth stopping that test?"

"Because he's vigilant about protecting Aiden at all costs." Maddy clenched her fists. "You know he runs experiments with

Aiden's blood once a month. He won't even share with me what he's doing."

Tamar gently unclenched Maddy's fist and wrapped it in her warm hands. "No. It's not fair. How can he run tests not subject to his own office's oversight, but you can't?"

Maddy took a deep breath and let it out slowly. "Because he's Kenneth."

"Can you rerun the tests with another resurrector?"

Maddy shrugged. "I'm not sure what it would tell me. I need another depositioner, really."

Tamar leaned in. "Take mine, anyway. Maybe you can find something between the two of us."

"Thanks, but Kenneth will slow down my lab for probably close to a week with this audit."

"That's too bad. Maybe you can run some kind of experiment outside the lab that involves two necromancers."

Maddy drummed the fingers of her free hand on the lab bench. "You know, maybe I can." She turned to Tamar. "No one's ever attempted to recreate how Kenneth and I raised Aiden. I've wanted to try, but Kenneth refused. Hell, he banned me from even trying when I was younger."

"Banned? He sounds a little heavy-handed."

Maddy waved her hand. "Overprotective is more like it. Since the accident and my illness, he's treated me and Aiden as fragile little kids. But it's a real unknown. Did we both really feed into Aiden's resurrection, or was it all Kenneth, and did something unrelated cause my condition? You and I could run some real tests."

"I don't know. It sounds like a risk to you," Tamar said.

Maddy sat forward. "It wouldn't be. I volunteer at a veterinary hospital to revive pets. I know I can handle that level of load. We could attempt to resurrect one together."

"Okay." Tamar smiled. "Sounds like some weird necromancer date, but I'm willing to try."

Maddy leaned in and kissed her cheek, feeling excited about her work again. Kenneth might be able to slow her down, but he couldn't stop her. She'd find a way to recreate what they did for Aiden, and if two necromancers were stronger together, she'd convince him to help her fully revive Aiden with another resurrection attempt. Maybe Tamar would help Aiden.

"One other thing I need to do." She opened a new record in her system and sent it to the printer. She left Tamar at the bench and went to her rack of blood samples, where she picked up the two vials of Aiden's blood. Kenneth wanted her to dispose of them before the audit. She understood why, but she needed these samples.

She remembered Judith's statement from earlier. Who was Kenneth to judge her work? She pulled out two new vials and slapped on the labels from the new record she created—Anonymous eight. She transferred Aiden's blood into the new vials and set them in a separate fridge. Then she disposed of Aiden's old vials. It was the sneakiest thing she'd done in years, but she was resolved to not just solve the mystery of how they'd resurrected Aiden but find a way to bring him out of his coma as well. For safe measure, she repeated the deception with a vial of Kenneth's blood as well—Anonymous nine.

She returned to the lab and took Tamar up on her offer to donate blood for her tests, but she'd also mark it as anonymous, along with a vial of her own. On Monday, she'd rerun the test with fully anonymous donors, right in front of Kenneth's auditors. Only she would know who each donor was.

With a smile, she terminated the prior test run with Aiden's blood and deleted it all from her system. Kenneth would assume that was the end of that set of tests. And what Kenneth didn't know wouldn't hurt him.

❖

Tamar walked into the veterinary hospital on Tuesday afternoon and marveled at how much it all felt like a human hospital. She'd lucked out so far, and her dog, Kalev, remained healthy and not in need of serious vet help. Maddy led them through to the back of the facility. The room had that same feel as the morgue where Tamar had her first deathbed deposition.

An older woman in blue scrubs waited for them, her gray hair pulled up under a surgical hat as she came to greet Maddy.

"We had one elderly dog pass away overnight. It came from the rescue shelter, and they signed a waiver allowing your experiment."

"Thanks," Maddy said. "This is my protégé, Tamar. She'll be participating in the experiment today, but we run it under my license."

The woman held out her hand. "Helen."

Tamar shook the offered hand. "Glad to meet you."

Helen opened one freezer door and pulled out the metal tray.

"That's a large-breed dog," Maddy said.

"Malamute mix, ninety-five pounds. Will that be a problem?" Helen asked.

"No, not at all," Maddy said. "Thank you again for accommodating us on short notice."

When the vet left, Maddy pulled up a stool and peeled back the sheet covering the dog. It really was big, with paws twice the size of Kalev's.

"Are you sure it isn't too large?" Tamar asked.

"No. Its size actually might help. We don't want to fully revive an elderly dog, and Kenneth hasn't given us the test results of your bloodwork yet."

Kenneth didn't do a lot of things, in Tamar's mind, except cause his sister grief. She remembered Jasmine Bunte's subtle distrust of Kenneth as well and began to think less and less fondly of Maddy's brother, for all he had kept her out of trouble for her unlicensed resurrection.

"Okay, let's pull out our injectors," Maddy said, returning Tamar's focus to the experiment.

Tamar put their bag on a side bench, took out two injectors, and handed Maddy the one that held Maddy's blood.

Maddy typed in the little calculator app on her phone. "Okay, based on the weight and the results we're looking for, let's start with my blood. I'll inject half of what I would normally use for a pet resurrection. Then you follow. Since we don't know how much you need, we'll start with small doses."

Tamar watched Maddy use a buzzer to shave a small section of fur off one leg. Maddy injected at the shaved site and then pulled out a stethoscope to listen to the dog. "No heartbeat." She lifted the dog's lids. "Minor eye movement. Your turn."

Tamar stepped up, measured her dose, and injected the dog. Even with her single, small dose, the dog stirred. "Crap on a cracker," she said as the dog's paws started moving. "Did I give him too much?"

Maddy listened with the stethoscope again. "Kenneth needs to give me the report on your blood. That dose shouldn't have been enough, but yes. We'll have to extract our energy."

After the last time, Tamar didn't look forward to this part. "Yeah. Your brother needs to cough up the test results."

"I can go first," Maddy said, pulling the extractor from her bag.

"No. Let me. I need the practice."

Not that she wanted the practice, but anyway…She took the extractor from Maddy's hand and pulled a small portion of the dog's blood. She looked at it and turned to Maddy. "Is this safe? I mean, it's not human blood."

"The extractor actually cleanses the blood and eliminates any pathogens. When it changes from blue to red, the cleansing is done, and it's technically an injector at that point. Same tool for both. In this case, the resulting xenoinfusion will cause an immune response in your body, similar to what you felt at the deposition. It's not harmful, just unpleasant."

Tamar nodded. "If I end up with furry feet, I'm blaming you."

Maddy laughed. "We'll have furry feet together, then, since I'll have to do the same thing once you finish."

Tamar jabbed the injector into her forearm before she could chicken out. Maddy stood next to her with an arm around her waist. Tamar felt as woozy as she had the last time. "I should have sat down."

Maddy slid off her stool and eased Tamar onto it. Tamar felt the tug of the dog trying to keep the energy, but it was much less than with a human. Just before it was over, she felt a different tug that made her lean into Maddy's arms. A tremor raced through her and felt as if it ran from the dog, through her, and into Maddy.

Maddy let go as if she'd been shocked and pulled back. "What did you do?"

Tamar sat up. "What you told me to."

Maddy shook her head and pressed forward to check the dog. "He's gone."

"That's the point, right?" Tamar stood and leaned against the freezers, feeling the drain from the extraction. "Why does it feel weird this time? I expected it to be less than with a human."

Maddy shook her head. "It shouldn't be worse. It also shouldn't have returned the dog fully to the deceased state."

"On the bright side, I guess you don't have to go through the extraction as well," Tamar said. "On the dark side, I just sucked in dog energy, and intellectually, that's just weird."

Maddy smiled. "Joking aside, you did more than that. You also severed my link to the dog, and that's something completely new."

Was that the strange sensation Tamar had felt during the extraction? "Great. Who doesn't love forging new ground?"

Maddy slid the dog back into the freezer. "Do you feel well enough to head out?"

Tamar stood up. "Yeah. It wasn't draining this time, just strange."

"You can tell me all about that feeling when we get home."

Tamar held open the door leading out of the vet morgue. "I can entertain you with the story on the drive home."

"No. I'll want to take notes. Copious notes," Maddy said.

Great. Who didn't want to be odd enough to warrant copious notes, Tamar thought.

❖

Maddy spent all of Wednesday at the lab dealing with Kenneth's auditors. She wasn't the most extroverted person, and after a day of nonstop interviews that felt more like an inquisition, exhaustion tugged at her. She really should go home, but with the auditors finally gone for the day, she was free to kick-start what she was calling the quad test in her lab notes. Her phone buzzed with a call from Kenneth, but she wasn't in any mood to talk to him, so she let it go to voice mail. She carefully left all personal details out of the anonymous donors listed so only she knew the four test subjects were her, Aiden, Kenneth, and Tamar.

She was surprised an hour later by a text on her phone.

Miss you.

She smiled at Tamar's text. *You're just bored.*

I can be bored and miss you at the same time.

True. Maddy checked her lab setup. *I have to wait another thirty minutes here.*

Maybe I can entertain you for thirty minutes?

Now, there was an offer that had Maddy thinking of possibilities that were entirely inappropriate for a lab setting.

Look out your window.

Maddy pulled off her blue-light-filtering glasses and glanced at the dark windows across from her lab bench. She couldn't see anything much with the internal lights glaring off the glass. She stepped closer and shaded her eyes from those lights. A solitary Jeep sat in the parking lot with a solitary figure waving up at her.

Brat. I'll meet you at the front door.

With a smile, Maddy made her way down to the lobby. She used the reflection of herself in the elevator doors to pull the scrunchie out of her hair and finger-combed it before the doors opened.

Tamar waved from the outside door, and Maddy opened it. "Brat."

"You mentioned that." Tamar stepped inside and handed her a warm cup.

"Coffee?"

"Cocoa." Tamar lifted her own cup.

They returned to Maddy's lab. "I just need to wait another twenty-five minutes for the first test to complete, and then I can set up the overnight one."

Tamar sipped her cocoa. "Sounds interesting."

"Boring, really, but I hope the results prove interesting."

They passed the time with Tamar finding more and more ridiculous animal videos online. Maddy nearly spat out her cocoa on one involving a baby rhino and elephant playing in the mud. "You love animals," she said.

"That I do."

Maddy held Tamar's hand, feeling its warmth. "I'm sorry about the vet work the other day."

"Don't be," Tamar said. "It's never easy to deal with death, but I know we weren't injuring the dog, and he would have been in pain if we'd fully resurrected him."

The lab timer beeped. "First test is done." Maddy slid off her stool. She fed the results as parameters into the next set and placed the blood samples into the CR-2000.

"That's a big beast," Tamar said. "What does it do?"

"It's our new DNA analyzer. It's my first test run with it."

Tamar laughed. "You sound like a kid with a brand-new toy."

Maddy held up the first test tray. "I am, and I finally have enough samples to run a DNA comparison across ten necromancers." She held up a second tray. "And this is a secondary run that includes, you, me, and—"

Tamar placed a finger on her lips. "And Anonymous eight?"

"And nine." Maddy kissed that finger and stepped back. "You're a fast learner."

"Does that make us Anonymous ten and eleven?"

"Very fast learner." Maddy placed both trays in the DNA analyzer.

"How long will it take?" Tamar asked.

"The ten-sample test will take a few days, but our four should come back by the weekend." By the weekend, she could have isolated the genetic difference between resurrectors and deathbed depositioners. And by next week, she could have the DNA markers identified for all necromancers.

She turned to walk back to the lab bench, but a wave of dizziness swept over her, and she lost her balance as her vision faded out. She felt rather than saw Tamar jump from her stool and wrap her arms around her, catching her and lowering her to the floor.

"What's wrong?" Tamar asked.

Maddy's vision returned. She stared into a pair of beautiful brown eyes and Tamar's worried expression. She wanted to just fall asleep in Tamar's arms, but embarrassment forced her to try to stand. Tamar helped her up and to the lab stool in front of her computer.

"Maddy, what just happened?"

Maddy recognized the familiar sudden weakness. "Kenneth's running his test on my blood."

"That's ridiculous. He should have the decency to let you know ahead of time."

Maddy rested her head in her hands. "He probably did. I ignored a call from him about an hour ago."

Tamar sat beside her with folded arms. "An hour isn't enough time. Why can't he schedule these tests in advance? And why do them at night?"

Maddy held up a hand. "Easy, Momma Bear. I asked him

to run tests at night so I could be at home and in bed when they start." He could still have given her more than an hour's notice, but she didn't want to feed Tamar's anger. She wanted Tamar and Kenneth to like each other, or at least get along.

Tamar put a hand on her arm. "Should I take you home?"

Maddy shook her head. "Give me a few minutes to start the test first."

Under Tamar's worried gaze, Maddy pulled up the control program for the DNA analyzer and set up the test runs. It took longer than it should have to get everything set up because her brain fog had taken over.

She finally clicked the start on the test programs and sagged on her stool. "Done."

"Good." Tamar stood up. "Where's your cane?"

Maddy pointed to her left. "In my office." She didn't want to be a burden to Tamar, but she was glad for the help.

Tamar returned with her raincoat, cane, and shoulder bag. "I put your laptop in here as well. It's not raining or cold, so I can just carry the coat."

Maddy accepted the cane. "Thanks."

Tamar looped Maddy's spare hand through her arm and led the way back to the elevator and into the Jeep. Maddy's eyes shut, and she drifted off to sleep before they made it out of the business complex.

❖

Tamar waited and fretted for most of Thursday as Maddy stayed asleep in her room until well past two o'clock. When she finally heard Maddy leave her bedroom and shuffle into the upstairs bathroom, she raced up the stairs with a mug of tea.

Luis met her at the landing. "I guess you have this covered," he said with a smirk.

"You're not the only nurse in residence," Tamar said.

He held up his hands. "Wouldn't get in your way, dearie."

Maddy shuffled out of the bathroom and looked at each of them. Her hair lay in a tangled mess, and her eyes had large dark circles. "Do I want to know what the two of you are up to?"

"I am pure innocence," Luis said.

Tamar nudged him with her free hand. "He's just going back to check on Aiden."

"Is there a problem?" Maddy asked.

"No, no." Tamar held out the mug. "I brought you tea."

Maddy gave her a tired smile. "Mind if I drink it from bed?" She turned and shuffled back into her room.

Tamar hadn't been in Maddy's room before. She took in the rose-painted walls with white trim and the queen-size four-poster bed. Then she placed the mug on the matching side table and pulled the tan blanket up around Maddy's shoulders as she lay down again.

"You know I can't drink the tea if you tuck my arms in," Maddy said with a slight grin.

"Sorry." Tamar mentally kicked herself. She wanted to take care of Maddy. Heck, as a trained hospice nurse, she knew how. But somehow, seeing Maddy so weak seemed to erase all her work skills and leave her a bumbling fool.

Maddy uncovered an arm and held Tamar's hand. "It's fine. Sorry that I'm exhausted today. I've been overdoing things lately, and it was bound to catch up to me."

Tamar blamed Kenneth for her fatigue but kept her thoughts to herself. "Can I do anything for you?"

Maddy patted the other side of the bed. "Keep me company for a bit?"

Tamar walked around the bed and curled up next to Maddy on top of the covers. "I could tell jokes."

Maddy chuckled. "Oh, please, no. I've heard your jokes. How about you tell me about the severing you did at the vet the other day."

"No notepad, though."

Maddy sighed. "No notepad. My brain fog today would make those notes useless anyway."

"Okay," Tamar said. "Once upon a time…"

"Once upon a time?"

"Hey, it's my story. I can tell it the way I like."

Maddy shook her head and curled herself so her face was just inches away from Tamar's.

Tamar swallowed the urge to kiss that face. "Once upon a time, an intrepid pair of necromancers rode out to uncover the mysteries of their profession."

"We're intrepid now?"

Tamar placed a finger on Maddy's lips. "If you keep interrupting, I'll never get the story out."

"Heaven forbid."

"Back to our intrepid necromancers. There they were, face-to-face with the rising specter of a zombie monster that would ravage the villagers if let loose on the population. So they chose to sacrifice all, for God and country…and necromantic research, and bring the monster down."

Maddy laughed. "You have a knack for the dramatic."

"That I do. Anyway, with magic extractor wands in hand, the apprentice looked into the beautiful brown eyes of her mentor for her approval." Tamar grinned at the growing blush on Maddy's cheeks. "Then she took the ultimate sacrifice and turned the extractor wand on herself."

"Very flowery, but a little low on the tangibles," Maddy said.

Tamar sighed. "Researchers. They take all the fun out of storytelling. Okay, so without the flowery details, when I injected myself with the dog's filtered blood, I felt the same tug I'd felt at the deposition at first. It was a quick feeling, like you said, less than with a human. But then it morphed. I could almost feel my link sever, but before it did, it sort of…wrapped itself around another link and severed them both, if that makes sense."

Maddy frowned. "I'll have to do some research."

"Of course," Tamar said with a smile.

"Of course." Maddy returned her smile. "This is something new, at least to me. I should talk to Kenneth."

"But maybe you won't?" Tamar didn't really want Kenneth involved in anything between her and Maddy. Not that she didn't trust him, but she was still angry about how his research affected Maddy.

Maddy cupped her cheek. "He is the necromancer marshal for the state. I should report this incident to him."

Tamar sat up. "Well, if you have to, then I want to try one more experiment first."

"Oh? Who's the intrepid researcher now?"

Tamar held Maddy's hand in hers. "We both are. You're in bed right now, thanks to Kenneth and whatever tests he runs on you but doesn't tell you about." And how that was fair to Maddy, Tamar didn't know. Or why Maddy felt she had to be open with her research when her brother didn't return the favor.

"To be unbiased, a combination of things likely led up to this chronic fatigue flare-up," Maddy said.

"Fine. But his tests were one of them. So, how would you like to become part of your own research study?"

Maddy chuckled. "You have no idea how many tests I've run on myself."

"Good. This will be just one more." Tamar lightly stroked Maddy's hand with her thumb. "Let me sever the link to Kenneth's test."

Maddy's eyes widened. "You can't be serious. It will mess up Kenneth's test cycle."

"Why not? It's just a test, and it put you in the bed. And maybe your dear brother will learn not to drain you so much and find someone else to test on. Heck, he's already using my blood, so he doesn't need yours."

Tamar was surprised that Maddy didn't say no right away

but seemed to mull over the idea. "He should need two tests to prove a potential new skill, right?" she added.

"I feel like I'm being manipulated," Maddy said. "How would you propose to do this?"

"Extract your blood, same as we did with the dog, and inject it in me. If it works, we know I don't have to be linked to the, um, test subject?"

Maddy laughed. "I'm a test subject now?"

"Just trying to talk the talk."

Maddy pulled herself up to a seated position. "Okay. You talked the right talk. Let's give it a try."

Tamar scrambled off the bed and, with Maddy's instructions, found an extractor pen in her bag. She sat cross-legged on the bed next to Maddy. "Okay, step one, extract your blood." She pulled up the sleeve of Maddy's pajamas and took a small sample, then placed a Band-Aid over the tiny pinprick.

"Step two—inject myself."

Maddy patted the bed next to her. "Sit here against the headboard. This makes you dizzy."

Tamar scooted closer to Maddy. "Okay, ready?"

"Ready."

Tamar injected her forearm with Maddy's processed blood. At first she felt nothing. She closed her eyes and concentrated. Then she felt a tug on her energy and pulled. The sensation of a thread being severed seemed to snap back into her consciousness, and she smiled. "I think it's working."

Then she felt a stronger link, more like a thick cord that pulled energy from Maddy. "There's another thread here, stronger than the last."

"Don't touch that!" Maddy said. "That's probably the link between me and Aiden."

Tamar tried to study the link but couldn't get much out of it. She let go of the connection and leaned back against the headboard. "How do you feel?"

Maddy sighed. "Honestly, about the same."

Tamar opened her eyes. "Sorry. I guess it didn't work."

"Maybe it did. You did feel something, right?"

"Yeah. It's hard to explain, but I felt like there were two connections to your energy, and I severed the smaller link."

Maddy leaned on Tamar's shoulder. "We'll need to investigate this further. For now, though, I need another nap."

Tamar rested her head on Maddy's. "You and me both."

Maddy scooted back down in the bed. "Plenty of room here."

Tamar looked down at Maddy's fragile expression and smiled. "That's an invitation I'm happy to accept."

She pulled the covers over herself and fell into a light doze next to the most beautiful woman in her life.

❖

Maddy did feel better that evening. She'd woken up alone, a little disappointed that Tamar wasn't still next to her. Instead, she found a handwritten note on the pillow.

Samantha is taking me out to dinner and a lecture. See you this evening.
  Love, Tamar

Maddy smiled as she ran her finger over that last part, then tucked the note in her bedside drawer and got up. She waited for the lightheadedness that usually came from standing when she had a fatigue flare-up, but it didn't come. She decided to take off her pajamas, even though it was already past seven in the evening.

The casual blue linen pants she selected felt soft against her skin, as did the light cream sweater she pulled on. Feeling better than she had in a few days, she ate a quick, light dinner and went upstairs to sit with Aiden for a time.

He looked much the same, though with a fresh shave, thanks to Luis's care. She pulled the rocking chair closer to his bed and held his cold hand.

"We learned something new today," she said. She'd started the habit of talking to him when she was still a teenager, and it was almost therapeutic for her. "Tamar has the ability to recognize and separate necromancy links to other people. I don't know yet how it works, but the more hopeful experiment was when she and I returned life to a test animal. Now, don't get all worried on me. I know how much you love animals. This was an elderly dog who had already passed. We couldn't fully revive him at his advanced age. It would have been too painful for the poor anima."

She heard the rumble of a car in the driveway and smiled. "That's probably Tamar." She leaned in as if sharing a secret. "She's special. I think you'd like her. I know I do. Maybe a bit too much for knowing her such a short time."

When the door downstairs opened, she heard Kenneth's voice instead of Tamar's and tried to push away her disappointment.

"I'm up here in Aiden's room," she shouted back to him.

His heavy tread sounded on the stairs, and then he rushed into Aiden's room. "What's wrong? What happened?"

She took in his frazzled state and expression and frowned back at him. "Nothing's wrong. Why are you in a panic?"

He ignored her and walked over to Aiden. "Luis!"

Luis appeared in the doorway, and Kenneth glared at him. "You should be checking his vitals, not playing some video game or whatever."

"Kenneth!" Maddy stood up. "Aiden is fine. Whatever has you in a state, don't take it out on him. Luis has been the best caregiver we've had for Aiden in years."

Kenneth ran a hand through his thinning hair. "Are you okay, then?"

She walked out of the room, taking her brother by the elbow. She had no idea really if Aiden could hear her when she talked to him, but even if there was the slightest chance, she refused to have him overhear an argument that was obviously brewing with Kenneth.

When they were downstairs in the front living room, she sat down on the sofa. "Okay. What's this all about?"

He slumped into the side chair. "I'm glad everyone is okay." He looked tired.

"Frankly, I expected you'd be madder about my upsetting your test results than some random worry about Aiden and my health conditions."

"Test results?"

"Maybe it hasn't shown up, or maybe your tests are complete." She leaned forward. "We learned something very interesting today." She went on to explain Tamar's ability to sever a necromancy link that wasn't her own.

Kenneth paled. "That's dangerous." He stood up and paced, his expression switching to outright anger. "I can't believe you would be so reckless. With your health and Aiden's."

Maddy crossed her arms. "I would never risk Aiden's life, and I'm getting tired of you insinuating that I would. You've already canceled my tests at my own lab, which, by the way, posed zero risk to our brother."

He stood facing out the dark front window. "I'm cutting your funding."

"What?" She stood up and grabbed his arm. "You can't do that."

He turned to her. "Yes. I can. I'm responsible for all necromancy in this state." He peeled her hand off his arm. "I could pull your license from you for what you're doing."

"The fuck you can. I'm as heavily involved in the laws and regulations running necromancy in this state as you are. I've written the drafts of half the laws you and I have pushed through. And I know very well that I have not crossed any legal lines here."

"What about ethical ones?"

She flinched, remembering Anonymous eight and the tests she was running on the side. Well, she could stop those tests if she wanted to. Meanwhile, her brother was being an ass, but fighting him wasn't the solution.

She took a deep breath. "Look, I don't even know what we're fighting about here. You're already auditing my lab. When the results are in, we can sit down and discuss next steps."

Headlights flashed across both of them as a car pulled up into the driveway. This time it had to be Tamar. "I'm tired. You're tired. Let's look at this all with clear heads in the morning. Can you stay the night?"

He shook his head. "I have a committee meeting tomorrow on legalizing necromancy use for its health benefits to the living."

She disagreed with him on that front but kept her thoughts to herself. "Okay. Later in the week. And I promise I won't try any new experiments until we talk."

He grabbed his jacket at the door. "I appreciate that. And I'm sorry for my outburst, but I worry about you and Aiden. I have to keep you both safe."

She smiled, giving him a quick hug. "Always the overprotective big brother."

He patted her cheek. "Someone has to look after you."

Tamar opened the door and glanced at them both. "Hi, Kenneth."

He glared at her. "You and I need to talk. I'll have my assistant set up an appointment."

Without another word, he pushed past Tamar and out the door.

Tamar watched him go. "What did I do?"

Maddy tugged at Tamar's arm to pull her inside. "Someone pissed in his cornflakes today."

Tamar laughed as she shut the front door. Maddy pulled her into the living room and showed her a special email.

Tamar's eyes widened. "Already?"

"Already," Maddy said. "You've been doing journeyman level work for the past week, so it makes sense to make it official. I didn't get a chance to print out the certificate itself."

Tamar wrapped her in a warm hug. "Thank you."

Maddy was glad to have her back and Kenneth gone. She'd managed to smooth over some of his anger, but she didn't much like the idea of Kenneth interrogating Tamar without her present. Knowing how her brother could steamroll over any perceived opposition, she'd make sure she was there when his interview happened.

Kenneth sometimes turned their respective research into a pissing contest, and she usually let him win because it was just easier.

Not this time. Not if he pulled Tamar into his competition.

CHAPTER TWELVE

Tamar met Representative Jasmine Bunte at the base of the broad steps of the statehouse. "I was surprised to get your call this morning," she said.

Jasmine shook her outstretched hand. "I'm glad you could make it on such short notice. I think you'll find this session to be of interest, as I mentioned on the call. Kenneth Wu will be presenting his proposal to extend the legal use of necromancy."

Tamar winced. "He's kind of mad at me right now."

"Oh?"

"I did something he didn't like, I guess. Maddy didn't go into the details."

Jasmine smiled. "Kenneth Wu has some very fixed opinions on many things. My advice? Be wary of crossing that man's path as much as you can. I don't wish to overstep my bounds here, but he can be, shall we say, excessive in his reactions to those who oppose him."

"Yeah. I get that vibe from him lately myself. I'll keep myself out of his crosshairs."

"Good plan." Jasmine led the way to the private elevators. "While this is a closed session, each representative on the committee is allowed to bring one observer."

"And you chose me?" Tamar asked.

"Yes. Not many adult necromancers don't have entrenched

opinions. From your background, I assume you still have some flexibility. As someone who's learning necromancy as an older adult, you bring an interesting perspective."

"That's the first time someone has called me an older adult," Tamar joked. "Not sure I like the feeling."

"Oh, you get used to it. People assume I'm much older than I am, but that does mean someone occasionally gives up their seat on the bus for me. Age, perceived or real, has its silver linings."

They entered a bustling committee room. Tamar gawked at the broad windows with elaborate wood carvings around the frames, as well as the old, paneled walls. They weren't the cheap stuff from the 1970s, but made of actual carved wood, likely a hundred years old or more. Jasmine led her to a row of seats toward the back, where Tamar sat as Jasmine made her way up to the raised set of seats that held the committee members. She watched Jasmine smile her political smile at her peers.

Moments later, Kenneth entered from a side chamber, along with his assistant, Jen. They took a bench to one side. Kenneth scanned the room, pausing a moment when he obviously saw her before continuing his broad sweep. She swallowed. From the look of things, this certainly wasn't going to endear her to him. Maybe this was a mistake, but she owed Jasmine for having put up with her required interview session earlier.

Tamar settled in as the session began. It felt a bit like a civics lesson as the committee started its slow process, with each member having to make opening statements as if they were all on C-SPAN. After they all had their little time in the limelight, the chairperson asked Kenneth to present his material.

He stood, dressed in a fancy navy-blue suit that looked hand-tailored. He had a smooth presentation style, taking in the committee members and their observers and assistants in the audience. He looked energetic, younger even, until Tamar realized the gray was gone from his temples. Hair dye? She sat straighter as he started his pitch.

"It's a scientific fact that necromancy skills go beyond the reviving of the deceased. From historical records, we know this has been the case for a century. It's actually a misnomer to label us all as necromancers. We are healers, healers who can break the grip of death in some instances, but still healers. What I propose is not something unique. Prior to the legalization of necromancy, we used our skills in private to help cure the sick before we had medicines to do this for us. But many illnesses don't respond to modern medicine. These are the illnesses we can apply necromancy to. We don't just revive the dead. We can heal the ill."

"An interesting perspective," one of the committee members said. "How do you propose we determine the legal boundaries?"

Kenneth stepped in front of his table and walked the room as if it were an audience he was entertaining. "The same way we do for necromancy today. We broaden the legal uses of necromantic blood. I'm proposing a new, entrepreneurial option. Years ago we took this step with marijuana, and it opened up financial success for many small businesses across the commonwealth."

"That success didn't extend to minority communities," Jasmine said. "But let's keep with your analogy. As I understand it, each use of a necromancer's blood takes its toll on the necromancer. How do you propose protecting them from exploitation?"

Kenneth waved his hand as if brushing the worry aside. "You well know, Representative, that necromancers are being exploited already in the black market. I simply propose that we open it up so they can establish their own businesses, legally."

Jasmine shook her head. "That doesn't explain how you protect them, Mr. Wu."

He widened his hands. "How do we protect anyone who lives by their physical skills? Think of it this way—we don't limit what prize pitchers can do in baseball. We let them push themselves to the limits. Sure, sometimes they develop career-ending injuries, but until then, they get to capitalize on their abilities. Some make millions."

"So you want to provide legal coverage for a person to sell their necromantic blood to the highest bidders?" Jasmine asked.

"Capitalism runs our economy," he said. "I'm asking that we let necromancers out of their legal cages and allow them to participate in our capitalist society as full members." He turned to the audience, and Tamar felt his gaze lock on her. "A licensed necromancer can use her skills for things beyond the obvious, things like helping ease the passing of the dying, or even giving the family a few precious more moments with a loved one."

He smiled, but Tamar didn't feel like his expression was meant for her. He had just reminded her of her precarious legal position as someone who had practiced necromancy without a license. Well, he could hold that over her all he wanted, but he was the one who had swept it all under his license at the car accident.

You have no proof, and even if you did, I can't be manipulated that way, she thought. She gave him a little wave, and her smile broadened when she saw his confused frown. Good.

He cleared his throat and continued his lecture, handling interruptions as if the legislators were all his pupils. The session went on for a full hour and a half, but by the end, Tamar could tell, even if Kenneth couldn't, that he hadn't won over most of the committee members yet.

Also good.

The session ended, and she followed Jasmine to her office. Tamar took in the worn look of the small space compared to the elaborate session chambers and wondered why her tax dollars weren't improving some of the representatives' offices. The paneling here was definitely from the seventies, and the little rusty radiator hissed at them as they entered.

"Well," Jasmine said. "Your thoughts?"

Tamar took the spare chair in front of Jasmine's old metal desk. "I don't like it. I mean, he's smooth with his presentation, but it just feels off to me."

"Can you elaborate that feeling?" Jasmine asked.

Tamar gazed out the window at the sliver of cloudy sky visible beyond the building. "It seems too easy to abuse. Sure, some necromancers would have the backing, financial or otherwise, to create their own business. But the rest of us? We'd be hired by some big corporation somewhere and likely never see that financial boon he's talking about. People like him would make all the money off the backs of other necromancers."

"Interesting," Jasmine said. "As he mentioned, people are already doing that, illegally."

"Right, but why make it legal? It won't help the average necromancer. In fact, I could see it pulling in those with less skills but more desperate financial needs and exploiting them even further."

Jasmine leaned back in her chair. "So what do you feel should be done about those setting up their own black market and trading necromantic blood to the highest bidders?"

Tamar shrugged. "It's illegal today, so they should be found and prosecuted."

Jasmine studied her a moment. Tamar had no idea what the other woman was thinking, but she wasn't going to change her opinion on the matter. And she knew Maddy agreed with her. They'd spoken about it when she told Maddy about the session invite.

Jasmine seemed to come to a decision. She pulled open a desk drawer and pulled out a small memory stick. She walked around the desk to stand next to Tamar. "I'd like your opinion on what's on this memory stick as well." She seemed almost apologetic. "It may not be easy to digest, but I think it's important for you to review it."

Tamar accepted the memory stick and put it in her pocket. "Sure."

"I look forward to your thoughts on the matter. You already have my cell phone number."

❖

Tamar wandered around the house in her slippers, a funk settling over her. Maddy had left early for work, and with it being the weekend, Tamar missed both her dog and her freedom to just go out and do things.

Well, that wasn't quite true. She hadn't had the most engaging social life before all this necromancy training started, and strictly speaking, she could go out and do things. No. What she really missed was Maddy.

You're well into sappy-land over her, she thought with a smile.

Luis came down the stairs as she wandered by. "Happy thoughts?" he asked.

She smirked. "What's not to be happy about today?"

He started counting on his fingers. "Cloudy and dreary. You're stuck here when you clearly have the energy to go home."

She hoped her expression didn't show the slight panic she felt at leaving this place, but his smirk said she'd failed.

He held up a final finger. "And last but not least, Maddy's off at work this morning."

She covered her eyes a moment. "I'm that transparent?"

"Like an open book, sweetie."

He patted her arm as he headed to the kitchen. "She's just as much an open book as you are."

Tamar didn't waste a moment but trailed him into the kitchen. "What do you mean?"

He put the kettle on for tea. "Oh, wouldn't you like to know?"

Tamar leaned against the counter. "Don't make me beg."

He laughed. "Oh, I'd pay money for that, but come on. Do you really not know how Maddy feels about you?"

"I mean, maybe?" They had kissed a few times, so that was promising.

"Let's just say, she hasn't spent so much time in this house in ages."

Tamar glared at him. "She has to be here to train me."

He just raised one dark eyebrow at her.

"Okay. Maybe she doesn't," Tamar said.

"Trust me, you have at least one of the Wu siblings wrapped around your pinkie."

Tamar laughed. "Okay. I know that's not Kenneth, for sure. He texted me at six a.m. that he wants me to meet him in Boston tomorrow."

Luis didn't respond, just watched her out of the corner of his eye as he prepared his tea. She wasn't the only open book in this house. "You have some opinions about the other Wu sibling?" she asked.

He shrugged. "Not my place to comment."

"Oh, for real? You comment on everything."

He poured milk into his tea. "Not on Kenneth."

Tamar thought back and realized that he did seldom talk about Kenneth, other than as an employer. She tried another tactic, by opening up herself on the subject. "Between you, me, and the lamppost, he's not my favorite Wu."

"Paint me surprised," Luis said with a smirk.

"Well, yeah, but even so. There's something about him that just seems, I don't know, too slick."

Luis watched her as he took his first sip, so she went on. "I mean, he runs these tests on Maddy's blood that really take it out of her."

"Not just her," he said. "Aiden's vitals took a dip the day you went into Boston for the committee meeting. Kenneth must have run his tests that morning."

Tamar frowned. "See? Why does he get to keep secret what he's doing, but Maddy has to live with a week-long audit? It seems to me like he's abusing his position."

Luis nodded. "You don't trust him."

There. It was out in the open. "I don't. Maybe I'm being overprotective of Maddy. Heck, she'd probably hate it if she knew."

"No," he said. "She needs someone to be overprotective of her."

"Kenneth seems to think he is."

"But you and I know better, don't we?"

Yes. She did know better. She trusted not just her instincts on this one, but the evidence as well. Whatever Kenneth was up to on his tests, they weren't worth the toll they took on his siblings.

"Not much we can do about it, I suppose. I can't imagine trying to convince Maddy to stop Kenneth's tests on her and Aiden."

Luis shook his head. "Probably not. Not without some hard evidence."

"Yeah, and not sure how to get that."

Then again, maybe she did have an idea. She had that memory stick from Jasmine that she hadn't looked at yet, but it suggested the representative saw her as an ally. That could come in handy, if she could convince Jasmine to start a state audit on the necromancer marshal himself.

She took a deep breath. "Okay. Maybe I'm getting carried away here."

"Or maybe you aren't."

She looked at Luis. "You know something."

He shrugged. "I don't know, but I have my doubts. Come with me."

She followed him back upstairs and into the room he used as an office. Monitors beeped and screens flashed with Aiden's vitals. Luis sat at his desk and pulled up a file on his computer. "I have a video feed into Aiden's room all the time. I also pipe it into a file to review in case I'm away for a time. The file is written over every twenty-four hours."

He fiddled more with his computer and then pointed the monitor to her. "You might find this interesting."

She leaned over his shoulder and watched the short video as Kenneth sat beside Aiden. He held an extractor in his hand and jabbed it into his own shoulder. The video cut off after that. "So he's giving his blood to Aiden to help him."

"Look again." Luis replayed the video.

"Sorry. I'm not seeing anything unusual."

"Look closely at the extractor. It's red."

She looked again, and sure enough, the tool was red, not blue. "Okay, so he used an injector by mistake. Maddy told me they basically do the same thing. The colors are so someone doesn't mess up."

"And do you think the necromancer marshal for the entire commonwealth of Massachusetts would mess up the color of the tool he used?"

Tamar leaned back. "What are you suggesting here?"

Luis folded his arms as if waiting for her to come to her own conclusion. She stared back at the frozen video, with the red tool, the injector tool, in Kenneth's hands. "You think Kenneth is juicing on his own brother's blood? That's pretty hard to believe and even harder to prove."

"Maybe." Luis went to a small fridge he kept for Aiden's medications. He pulled out a red injector. "I'm responsible for the disposal of all biological waste here." He held it between his fingers. "I just so happened to not dispose of this one."

Tamar glanced at the used injector. "You think a blood test would prove whose blood was in that tool."

He nodded. "I don't have the facilities to test it."

"But Maddy does." Tamar ran a hand through her unruly curls, likely making them an even bigger mess than usual. "Do you know what you're asking here?"

He placed the injector into the back of his fridge. "It's here whenever you need it."

Need it? Crap. This was too much to take in. She shuffled from Luis's office to her own bedroom and lay flat on the covers. Way too much to take in.

❖

Maddy spent many Saturdays at her lab, but she'd rather have spent this Saturday at home with Tamar. Thanks to Kenneth's week-long audit, though, she had to get back in to work and put her projects back on track. He wouldn't release the audit details until Monday, but she was confident he'd find nothing to derail and everything he needed to compete with her lab on the next set of federal grants they were both shooting for.

"Not playing fair," she grumbled to herself as she stepped off the elevator and into her corner office. First things first. She put down her bag, pulled off a light jacket, and went to the break room to start the coffee. She stared out the break room window at the dreary, overcast day while the coffee percolated. She could have made a single cup, but she'd need a few to get her through the morning.

Back in her office with a steaming mug, she turned on her computer and scanned emails from her lab team before digging into which projects she needed to restart. She read and she sipped.

She finally came to the project she was most interested in. "Good old Anonymous eight." The tests run on her blood, Kenneth's, Aidin's, and Tamar's had finished the night before. She lifted her mug for another sip of coffee and glared at its emptiness. Experienced at delayed gratification, she left the project report unopened while she fetched another fresh mug of coffee. This report would make the whole annoying audit week a dim memory and cheer her up for sure.

Ready once again at her desk, she pulled up the test results and started reading.

She felt a frown growing on her forehead. "This doesn't make sense."

The deeper she scanned the results, the deeper her frown

grew, until finally, she went to the DNA analyzer itself and pulled out the test trays. She checked each tray to verify each matched the blood samples she intended.

"No. I didn't make a dumb mistake," she said to herself. So why were the results a mess? She went back to her desk and read them again. It should have been a straightforward test. It had four known samples that should have been in pairs. She and Aiden should have shown similar markers for limited resurrection, while Kenneth and Tamar should have shown some kind of match for the strong resurrection skills they both had.

Instead, the results said, basically, next to nothing. Her theories on necromantic blood markers were shot to hell. She rested her head in her hands, frustrated at not just the test results, but the risk she'd taken by using Aiden and Kenneth's blood samples as mislabeled anonymous donors. "All for nothing."

Disappointment sank deep into her, but she brushed it aside for the moment when her phone buzzed. She picked it up to see a text from Tamar.

Kenneth wants me to meet him in Boston tomorrow.

Addled, it took a moment for Maddy to realize what that was about—Kenneth's interview with Tamar. The hell she would let that happen at his convenience.

He can come to the house. I'll take care of it.

She felt a thrill when Tamar responded with a heart emoji. When had she become so fond of Tamar that a simple emoji could set her pulse racing for a moment? With a smile erasing her earlier frown, she sent Kenneth the details on meeting at the house for lunch on Sunday. Better to not give him the option of picking a time and place to grill Tamar.

Maddy wanted to just close down her computer and head home, but she had hours' worth of report reviews to get through and two tests she could restart now that the audit was over.

With a not-so-fresh mug of coffee, she settled back into a long morning's work.

❖

A walk along the beach always cleared Tamar's head, but this Sunday morning, it wasn't working its usual magic. Between the pending meeting with Kenneth and Luis's little injector bomb, she couldn't settle down. She finally sat back at the fire pit and just watched the waves lap the shoreline. A lone seagull flew overhead, obviously hoping she had some food, but when she didn't move, even it gave up and left her to her own thoughts.

Her phone buzzed in her pocket, and she pulled it out to see a message from Maddy.

Kenneth's here. Are you ready to get this over with?

If only she knew what this really was.

Yeah. On my way.

She walked slowly back to the house and left her sandy shoes in the sunroom. She found Maddy and Kenneth in the green room.

"There you are," Kenneth said, with a broad smile that didn't even pretend to show in his eyes.

Tamar returned an equally false smile, but the smile turned real when she accepted Maddy's offer to sit next to her on the sofa. The two of them hadn't had a chance to talk yet, since Maddy had worked late the night before. She wasn't sure what she'd say to Maddy right now, so instead she turned back to Kenneth.

"You wanted to talk to me about something?" she asked.

"Right to the point," he said. "Fine. I think your recovery from the accident is complete. Your test results prove it."

"I'd like to see those test results," Maddy said.

Kenneth's smile slipped some. "Well, that's confidential information."

"I haven't seen them either," Tamar said. "Since they're my test results, I should have access to them."

Kenneth shrugged. "I'll see that they're sent to you, but

they aren't any big secret. We're talking basic blood work here. Your white blood cell count was high after the resurrection, but that's returned to normal. And based on your exercises out on the beach, you're physically fit enough to return to work."

Well, that wasn't so bad, she thought. She'd been getting bored hanging around the house when Maddy was off at work anyway.

"So I'll be terminating your short-term disability qualification starting tomorrow."

"Why not wait until next Monday?" Maddy asked.

"I'm sure she's eager to get back to work and to her own apartment," he said.

And that was the real reason. He wanted her out of the house, fast. Now Tamar wondered why.

"Fine," Maddy said. "She returns to work, but she stays here as long as she wants." Maddy turned to her. "It makes her training easier."

Tamar smiled. "Yes. That sounds good to me."

It didn't sound good to Kenneth, if his blank expression was any indication. He smiled, again, and Tamar couldn't help the icy feeling down her own spine at that grin.

"That sounds reasonable, for now. It also makes it easier to get your blood samples for more tests. Maddy tells me you have some unique skills we should investigate further."

Unique skills? She turned to Maddy, who wouldn't look her in the eye. So Maddy must have shared some of their training results with Kenneth. Shoot. She wished that hadn't happened.

"As this is something we haven't come across before, I'm moving that aspect of your training under the office of the necromancer marshal. We don't want any lawsuits coming from unforeseen side effects, do we?" he said with a wink and a smile.

Maddy glared at her brother, but Tamar could tell she didn't have a ready response to Kenneth's obvious power play.

Tamar sat up straighter. Time to take control of her own

destiny here. "For now, I plan to avoid exercising that unique trait, as you call it. I want to complete my training with Maddy and get my license."

Kenneth nodded with a look of triumph. "Good decision."

The rest of the conversation drifted to medical and research topics. Tamar's mind wandered as they talked, but she could tell something was bothering Maddy and wanted to shove Kenneth out the door so she could find out what.

Kenneth didn't leave until after lunch, which meant an extra hour of smiling and pretending he wasn't getting under her skin. Tamar thought she hid that well, until he left, and Maddy turned to her from the kitchen table.

"Okay. What gives?" Maddy asked.

Tamar's felt her eyes widen. "I'm sorry?"

Maddy pointed one finger at her. "You, my sweet, are an open book. It's one of the traits I love about you, but it also means I know exactly when you're hiding something, because you just don't hide it well."

Tamar tried to concentrate on schooling her expression but couldn't stop the grin that Maddy's words caused. "So, there are things you love about me?"

Maddy blushed. "Let's not change the subject. I could cut the tension between you and my brother with a knife."

"I could say the same thing about the two of you. Do you two always engage in a test of wills?"

Maddy sighed. "More often of late, it seems."

Tamar took the opportunity in front of her to keep the subject on something other than her growing distrust of Maddy's brother. She stood up and offered her hand to Maddy. "How about tea in the sunroom, and you can tell me what's going on. You've been down since last night."

Maddy took her hand and stood. "That sounds great."

"Head that way, and I'll bring our mugs," Tamar said.

Settled once again on the sofa that faced the wide sunroom windows looking out on the beach, Tamar tossed a blanket over both their laps as they cuddled closer. "Did something go wrong at work yesterday?"

Maddy nodded. "My test results. You remember the tests I was running against your blood, mine, Aiden's, and Kenneth's? Well, they came back a mess."

"How so?"

"You and Kenneth are strong resurrectors. I'd wager yours is even stronger than his. My skills are weaker by far. I can resurrect small animals, but humans, at least after the accident with Aiden, are beyond me. And then Aiden himself could never go beyond deathbed depositions. My research has to date isolated a couple of markers in necromancer blood, so I ran tests specific to those markers."

"And?" Tamar sipped her tea as she listened.

"If my markers were correct, I'd see a direct correlation between the strengths of each of us and the blood markers. What I saw made no sense. You and Aiden have similar markers, as do Kenneth and I."

"So what does it mean?"

Maddy sighed and turned to look out the window. "It means what I thought I isolated in the blood markers is incorrect. It means my hypothesis for the past year is wrong."

"Oh." Tamar put her arm around Maddy. "So it's back to the drawing board?"

Maddy leaned into her to rest her head on Tamar's shoulder. "Not completely, but close enough. Kenneth's audit shut down multiple active test runs, but that's probably for the best if my hypothesis is so far off the mark."

"Maybe there are other markers as well. I mean, you found some, but maybe there's an interaction between them that makes up the relative differences between necromancers."

"Maybe." Maddy wrapped herself closer, her arm around Tamar's waist. "Maybe I just need a break."

Tamar chuckled and kissed the top of Maddy's head. "But you're not going to take one, are you?"

Maddy growled, and Tamar felt that rumble all the way to her toes and back. "Maybe I can take your mind off work for a bit."

Tamar gently lifted Maddy's head and stared into her beautiful brown eyes. She leaned near and pressed her lips to Maddy's. The cuddle turned more romantic, more urgent.

Work, Kenneth, everything took a back seat to her and Maddy and the growing attraction between them.

CHAPTER THIRTEEN

Tamar sat cross-legged on the kitchen chair with her phone pressed to her ear. "Yes, Nanna. I'll be there before sunset tomorrow night for Yom Kippur. I promise."

"Bring Maddy with you if you like," Nanna said. "She's a lovely girl."

Tamar smiled. "I think so, too. I'll ask, but she may not feel comfortable with an all-day fast."

"She doesn't need to, but I understand. See you tomorrow, then."

Tamar ended the call and stretched out from her cramped position. Maddy had already left for work, and as much as she hated agreeing with Kenneth, it probably was time for her to come off disability and get back to her job as well. She couldn't bring herself to start that process, knowing it would separate her some from Maddy. Instead, she went up to her bedroom and pulled out her laptop.

"Time to see what Jasmine gave me," she said to herself, finding the memory stick the representative had handed her before the weekend.

Tamar plugged it in and scanned the contents. She gave credit to Jasmine, or perhaps one of her staff, for the way the files were organized. They were in separate folders with interesting names like Illegal Blood Trade and Global Necromancy Market

Trends. But what caught her eye and the first folder she clicked on was the one named Wu Family.

Within that folder were two subfolders marked Twins and Madeline. Tamar smirked, knowing Maddy hated her full name. She couldn't help but click on that folder first. With a smile and a slight twinge of guilt, she flipped through pictures of a young Maddy, full of bright smiles. Also included were a few newspaper articles about the surfing accident and Aiden's death and resurrection. The other files went deeper into Maddy, and when she saw what seemed like Maddy's private medical reports, she shut down that file. It was more information than anyone should have, especially Maddy's political opponent. Tamar didn't understand why Jasmine had it, but she intended to let Maddy know.

Feeling guilty about invading the family's privacy, she flipped instead and read through the other two main folders. When she finished those, she couldn't help but open the Wu twins folder. She was so absorbed in her reading, she didn't notice Luis knocking on her open door. She looked up as he stepped closer and waved his hand in front of her.

"I said, did you want anything? I'm heading out to the grocery store," he said.

"Oh, ah, no thanks."

He pointed to her laptop. "That must be some fascinating reading."

She laughed. "Jasmine Bunte gave me a memory stick full of goodies last week. She has some stark evidence of a growing black market in necromancy blood, but she also has Kenneth's preliminary write-ups on legalizing that trade in blood for people who aren't dead."

Luis raised his eyebrows. "He wants to turn it all into a moneymaking business."

"Not him alone, either. He has links to a biotech company ready and willing to process and sell it when it becomes legal."

"Rich people have to make themselves richer," he said with a sigh. "Not sure how you can get so deep reading all that. Sounds dull to me, but to each their own."

Tamar laughed. "No, that was dull reading, but Jasmine's been collecting a lot of information on the Wu family. I was reading about the twins." She kept quiet about Maddy's details, as they seemed invasive.

"What's so interesting about them?" he asked.

Tamar leaned back to stretch the kink out of her back from slouching over her laptop for so long. "It's hard to put my finger on it, but it's the way all these reports talk about Kenneth and Aiden when they were younger. Kenneth was the shy, reserved one and Aiden the smooth talker. I guess Maddy's right. After the accident, Kenneth took on some of Aiden's characteristics."

She flipped through the files and pulled up one report from Aiden's high school. "See, even back then, Aiden was caught selling his blood to the high school football team. Nothing in the school rules kept them from doping up on necromancer blood, so the team got off, but Aiden was charged and suspended for a week. I don't know how Jasmine found his juvenile court records, but he was convicted of a crime for that and spent the next year reporting to a case worker."

"Wow. That's hard to grasp. Not that I'm familiar with Aiden's personality. I've known him only in his current state," Luis said.

"Yes, and now Kenneth's trying to legalize that type of behavior and turn it into a business."

"Maybe you're right," Luis said. "Maddy said he'd taken all Aiden's old stuff after the accident. His laptop, books, even paperwork."

Tamar frowned. "His way of coping?"

Luis shrugged. "Who knows?"

Luis left, and Tamar returned to the Wu twins files. She found a handful of videos of the twins when they were younger and wondered how Jasmine had acquired those. The woman had an enviable set of resources for digging deep into other people.

Tamar watched the first couple of videos in hopes of seeing a young Maddy in them. They focused mostly on the twins as early teens, playing basketball and surfing. Kenneth really wasn't a great surfer, at least not at that age. Aiden definitely came out on top in that competition and didn't seem to be a graceful winner. He taunted Kenneth in the video with a telltale wink and smile.

Tamar sat up straight. That wink and smile. She rewound the video and played it again and again. Then she played all the videos present. Not once did Kenneth give that wink. In fact, it seemed he glared at Aiden whenever his twin gave him that because it was obviously a taunt.

So why would Kenneth take on that characteristic from his twin if he clearly hated it as a teen?

This was beyond her understanding, but this seemed important. She batched up some of the files and her thoughts and emailed them to Samantha. If anyone could analyze the results, her cousin could, as a juvenile psychology specialist.

The last file she opened ended up being Aiden's juvenile record, complete with mug shot and fingerprints.

That gave Tamar an idea. She hopped on Amazon, and sure enough, she could get a kid's fingerprint kit delivered overnight. She felt self-conscious pressing the order button, but that niggling feeling that something was off between the twins just wouldn't leave her. Her order gave her a clear way to prove or disprove her worries. She had it delivered to her apartment in case she changed her mind overnight.

Now she just had to wait and stew.

❖

Maddy finished her second slice of the pizza that Tamar had ordered for dinner and struggled to keep the conversation going.

Tamar was, well, fidgety was the best description she could think of, especially after she read something on her cell phone. Maddy put her napkin down on the kitchen table. "Did you get bad news? Is something wrong?"

Tamar flinched. "No. Everything's fine. How was your day?"

"You asked me that already, and I answered already." Maddy reached across the table and took Tamar's warm hand in hers. "Something's bothering you."

Tamar gave her a weak smile. "Still that open book to you?"

"Wide open." Maddy waited, but she could tell Tamar wouldn't talk about whatever was concerning her, so she decided to change the subject. "I have something for you."

She went to her briefcase, pulled out her surprise, and handed it to Tamar.

Tamar read the piece of paper and looked up at her with wide eyes. "My training is done?"

Maddy nodded. "Done. All you need to do now is take the licensing exam, and you'll be a licensed necromancer."

To Maddy's surprise, Tamar didn't seem enthusiastic. She took Tamar's hand and led her into what was turning into their favorite room. Maddy had even started calling it the green room as well.

Once settled on the sofa, Maddy asked the obvious question. "Do you not want to be licensed anymore?"

Tamar's eyes widened. "No. I do."

"I expected a little more enthusiasm about your training being done."

Tamar looked down. "I am excited. And I'm grateful for all you've done for me."

"But?"

Tamar looked back at her. "But that means I have no excuse to stay here anymore. With Kenneth canceling my disability and all. I mean, I agree with him that I'm healthy and can get back to work. It's just…"

Maddy took Tamar's face in her hands, staring into deep-brown eyes she could get lost in. She leaned near until their lips met. Their kiss started slowly but built into an almost frantic expression of what they felt for each other.

Breathless, she pulled back, her forehead pressed against Tamar's. "I don't want you to leave."

Tamar gasped. "I don't want to."

Maddy smiled and sat up straight. "Well, that's easily resolved. You don't leave. Or, if this isn't the place, we could go to my apartment. Or," she added shyly, "yours, if you prefer."

Tamar wrapped her in a hug. "Anyplace that has you in it is perfect to me. I hope you like dogs."

Maddy laughed. "I hope you like tortoises."

Tamar pulled back. "A tortoise named Donatello? How could I not love it?"

"It was Aiden's. Kenneth was going to keep it, but I fought him for it. He still holds a grudge, but our parents agreed I would take it since Kenneth had always hated it, up until Aiden's accident."

Tamar stuffed her hands between her knees and stared at the floor. Maddy didn't know what she'd said, but something seemed to upset Tamar. She put a tentative hand on Tamar's back. "What is it?"

Tamar shook her head. "Just something working through my brain." She turned back to Maddy. "It's not you, or us, I promise."

"Can you talk about it?"

Tamar stared at her hands. Could she talk about it? Was it too soon? She had Samantha's quick assessment of the information she'd sent her cousin earlier, and it was chewing away inside her. She owed it to Maddy to be open. If they were considering a real relationship, honesty and trust mattered.

"Do you ever feel like Kenneth really isn't…himself?" she asked.

Maddy gave her a one-eyebrow raise. "How do you mean?"

"Well, you said before he was an easygoing guy as a teen, definitely not the political type he seems to be now."

Maddy stared out the dark window. "Yes. He changed a lot after the accident."

"Changed to be more like Aiden." Tamar didn't post it as a question, and Maddy didn't disagree. "That's kind of a big change, don't you think?"

"I suppose. We all coped with the accident in different ways. That's the way Kenneth coped. My parents wanted him to go to therapy, but he refused."

I bet, Tamar thought. "He's also very secretive about his so-called tests on his brother's blood."

Maddy turned to her. "Is that what's bothering you? You don't have to agree to have your blood tested by him. I'm sorry if I didn't make that clear earlier."

Tamar shook her head. "No. It's not that." She wasn't handling this well by trying to tease around the edges of what was on her mind. She took a deep breath. "Okay, so Jasmine Bunte sent me a bunch of files. Some of it was about the black-market trade in necromancer blood."

Maddy pulled back. "Jasmine. What's she up to?"

"Background info to counteract Kenneth's push to legalize more uses for necromancy," Tamar said. "Did you know Aiden got into trouble for selling his blood to his high school football team?"

Maddy's eyes widened. "No. I didn't. I was probably too young for my parents to share that information with me at the time." She frowned. "How did you find out?"

Tamar stood up. "I'll be right back." She ran upstairs and grabbed the memory stick from her desk. She'd already downloaded it all to her laptop anyway.

Back downstairs, she handed the stick to Maddy. "That's everything Jasmine gave me. Fair warning, some of it seems invasive for sure. But it includes Aiden's juvenile record."

"That bitch." Maddy stared at the memory stick in her palm. "She's taken her distrust of necromancers too far this time."

Tamar placed her hand over Maddy's. "Maybe not." She felt Maddy flinch under her hand, but now that she'd started, she wouldn't stop. "There's more there, more than I think even Jasmine is aware of."

Maddy looked at her, brown eyes seeming so trusting Tamar's heart nearly broke. "What if the accident happened differently from what you remembered?"

"What?"

"Okay, so from what you've hinted at and what Jasmine has in those files, Kenneth was a very different person as a teen. Shy, focused on his schoolwork, definitely not outgoing. Aiden was the sly one, the operative, sneaky, competitive."

"Yes, yes. I know all that."

Tamar closed her eyes a moment. In for a penny. "I sent some of the files to my cousin Samantha. She's an expert in the field of teen psychology."

Maddy pulled her hand free. "You sent private details of my family to your cousin?"

"I'm sorry. I had to. Look, something is off with Kenneth. Samantha agrees, based on what I sent her, that someone like a surviving twin might take on some of the characteristics of the other, but never to this extreme. Not without some deeper psychological problem present."

Maddy folded her arms. "So, based on some memory stick and a dime-store analysis by your cousin, you think my brother is deranged?"

This was not going well at all, but Tamar didn't know how to stop. "No. I think it's something worse."

"What could be worse?"

In for a pound. "I think Kenneth is Aiden."

"What?"

"I think the man in the bed upstairs is Kenneth."

Maddy stood up. "That's the most ridiculous thing I've ever heard."

Tamar talked faster. "It all makes sense, if you switch them. Aiden is political. He had the motivation as a teen that Kenneth never had. Ask yourself—which of the two would you think would become the youngest state necromancer marshal in the country? Which would want to legalize more uses of necromantic blood to turn a business profit?"

"I told you," Maddy said. "Kenneth took on Aiden's goals. It's his way of making up for not being able to fully resurrect his brother."

Tamar shook her head. "Then why is Kenneth injecting himself with Aiden's blood?"

"No. You have it wrong. It's the other way around. Kenneth regularly tries to boost Aiden with his own blood. I offered mine as well, but Kenneth refuses to let me."

"No. Your own tests prove my point. My blood, resurrector blood, matches the markers for the man in the bed upstairs. Not yours, not your surviving brother. His matches yours…weak resurrectors."

Maddy folded her arms. "No."

Tamar stood and placed a hand on Maddy's arm, but Maddy stepped out of her reach. Tamar couldn't stop the tears forming in her eyes. "I'm sorry, Maddy. If you don't believe me, there's a blood injector upstairs that Kenneth used the other day. Have it tested."

Maddy whipped around to face Tamar. "You kept Kenneth's injector? That's unethical."

Tamar didn't mention it came from Luis. She wouldn't risk his job based on her own theories, even if he might agree. "I saw him inject himself with it after extracting from the man upstairs. I know I shouldn't have taken it out of the biohazard waste, but we need to determine which twin is which."

"No. We do not. I know my brother. He's Kenneth." Maddy turned to pick up her cane and started out of the room. "Maybe he's right. Maybe it is time for you to get back to your own work. Your own life."

CHAPTER FOURTEEN

Maddy woke up Tuesday morning with a stress headache and aching joints. For once, she knew the weather wasn't causing her symptoms to flare up. No. Last night's fight with Tamar and then watching her pack her few belongings and drive off had put Maddy into a tight knot of stress that spiraled into insomnia overnight and left her drained and unwilling to get out of bed.

She checked her phone for the fourth time and saw multiple messages from Tamar. A part of her wanted to rush up and apologize for the fight, but another part of her wasn't ready to forgive Tamar for her horrible insinuations. She left the messages unread as she crawled out of bed and into the shower.

After a good hot soak, she didn't feel any better but forced herself downstairs for breakfast. The house felt quiet, empty, even though only Tamar had left. With a plate of toast and a cup of coffee, Maddy sat at the kitchen table to force herself to eat.

Her phone buzzed, and she glanced at the incoming call from Kenneth. With a sigh, she picked up her phone.

"Not a good day," she said.

Kenneth chuckled. "Rough night?"

Maddy felt her eyes moisten and was glad this wasn't a video connection. "Tamar left."

"That's a good thing, isn't it?" he asked. "She was ready to get back to work. Glad to hear she took that step on her own."

Maddy winced. "It wasn't quite on her own. I sort of asked her to leave." She had regretted that move many times in the night but still couldn't let go of the accusations.

"Did something happen?" Kenneth asked.

"She had some daft accusations. Crossed a line I didn't even realize was there."

"What did she say?"

Maddy heard the seriousness in Kenneth's voice. She didn't know why he cared but recognized by the tone that he wouldn't let this go. He was more like Aiden in that regard.

Shit. She was even mixing up the two of them now, just like Tamar had. She needed to break that habit, fast. "It started with our favorite representative."

"Jasmine Bunte. She's a pain in my ass. What did she do this time?"

"She gave Tamar a bunch of private details about our family." Maddy had left the memory stick up in her bedroom, not willing to look at it yet.

"Good," Kenneth said. "If Bunte crossed a line, we can get her up on charges."

"Maybe," Maddy said. "I didn't think it was possible to open juvenile records."

Kenneth was quiet for a time. "What records?"

Maddy sat up. "Aiden's. I assume you knew he sold his blood to the football team in high school."

Kenneth didn't say anything, so Maddy continued. "I'm sure there's more horrible stuff on that memory stick. I haven't read it myself. I only know what Tamar mentioned from it."

"Don't read it. Don't do anything with it," Kenneth said. "It's evidence now."

"Okay, fine." Maddy lowered her head into her hand. "Tamar took whatever she read and spiraled off into space with it. She went so far as to accuse you of some kind of deep psychosis or something. That you took on all of Aiden's character." She couldn't bring herself to mention how extreme Tamar's views were. Kenneth already sounded angry enough without hearing that.

"I should never have trusted Tamar," Kenneth growled. "I want that memory stick."

Maddy glanced at the microwave clock. "I need to get to work. Did you want to come by tonight?" She could do with the company.

"I'll be there in an hour," he said.

After he hung up, Maddy went back upstairs to get the memory stick. She held it in her hand, then decided to copy it to her laptop first, in case something happened to the original. She was beyond pissed off at Jasmine for this invasion of privacy and joined her brother in hoping they could bring a legal case against her. She knew it wasn't fair, but she blamed Jasmine for ruining her relationship with Tamar.

Tears came then, tears she'd been too angry to shed during her sleepless night. Tamar was gone, and with her went Maddy's hopes for love.

❖

Tamar sat on her own sofa, nibbling at a slice of toast and knowing she should be eating more before the Yom Kippur fast started that night. She had no appetite, though, not since leaving Maddy's place. She'd woken up with a dull headache and a more painful heartache. She'd ruined everything, and for what? Some ridiculous notion that Maddy's brothers had switched identities. What was she thinking?

She pulled out her phone, ready to text yet another apology and this time claim, what? A sudden brain tumor made her say those things to Maddy? No. She didn't have any good excuse for what she'd done other than falling under Jasmine's spell of general distrust of Kenneth, then taking it to a foolish level on her own.

The doorbell rang, breaking Tamar out of her funk long

enough to leave the sofa and answer it. She walked out and opened the door. No one was there, but a box sat on the front stoop with her name on it. She was halfway up the stairs before she remembered what she'd ordered.

She opened the box on the kitchen table and pulled out the Junior Detective kit she'd bought the day before. There it sat, with a cheesy magnifying glass and notebook, but also a functional fingerprint kit, complete with a downloadable phone app to compare two sets of prints.

Her phone buzzed with a call from Samantha.

"It's too early to bug me about tonight," Tamar said.

"Hello to you too, you grumpy sod. Who pissed you off today?" Samantha said.

Tamar rested her head in her hand. "Me."

"Explain."

Tamar told Samantha everything—well, everything except the silly fingerprint kit on her table.

"You know how to make an impression," Samantha said. "What will you do now?"

"I don't know. I really burned that bridge behind me with Maddy."

"For good reason," Samantha said. "Whatever is really going on there, it's not what it seems on the surface for sure. You're better off out of that place."

Was she really? Maddy had become so much a part of her life, thinking that romance was over made her unable to function. Yet, as she fingered the detective kit, she realized she hadn't made her accusations in a vacuum.

Well, if she burned that bridge, she should do it with solid evidence.

"Gotta go," she said.

"Oh, I don't like the sound of that. What are you planning?" Samantha asked.

"Nothing you'll agree with," Tamar said.

"You're right. If you can't even tell me what you're planning, I definitely don't agree with it, Tamar."

"I need to resolve this mess. Don't worry. I'll still be at Nanna's by sunset." She checked her phone. She had four hours easily before she needed to head out to Western Massachusetts. Four hours to prove to herself whether her ideas were out in space or not.

She pulled herself up and into the shower. She had things to do today. They might not repair her lost relationship with Maddy, but they would either clear up a very old wrong or disprove her theories entirely, and then she could give Maddy a full apology for the accusations against Maddy's family.

❖

Tamar pulled up to the Wu family house shortly after two o'clock. Luis met her at the door. "I'm trusting you to take only what's yours," he said.

Tamar had given him the excuse that she'd left some of her belongings behind but didn't want to show up while anyone else was home. He'd texted her after Maddy and Kenneth had left.

"I need to get some supplies," Luis said. "Lock up when you're done, and leave the keys in the sunroom."

"Sure." She watched as he drove off in the gray van they used whenever they needed to transport Aiden to the hospital. After the van disappeared down the gravel drive, Tamar jogged up the stairs and straight into the room with Aiden. Or Kenneth, if her theory proved right.

She pulled out her cell phone and opened the Junior Detective app. It linked into the phone's own fingerprint-identification capabilities, and she started imprinting each of Aiden's fingers. It took longer than she expected, but it was hard to get someone else's fingers to line up on the phone properly. After twenty minutes of fussing, she'd managed to log all the prints.

She could leave, but instead, she sat by his bedside and scanned in the prints from Aiden's juvenile record and set the detective program to process them both. Two short minutes later, she stared at the results with her mouth hanging open. For all she'd convinced herself of this body-swapping theory, she hadn't really prepared herself for the answer.

Zero match.

Zero.

The man in the bed was not Aiden Wu.

"I thought you were kicked out of the house already."

Tamar turned around to see Kenneth in the doorway. No. Not Kenneth. She knew that now. It was Aiden. Aiden Wu. Her mind flitted between panic and anger. With a quick set of keystrokes, she sent the detective kit results to Samantha and then stood up.

She glared at the person in the doorway. "Why'd you do it?" She couldn't help herself. It all fit so easily in her mind now, his personality tics that were Aiden's, his career goals that were Aiden's. Even down to the "grayness" to his skin tone that Tamar had seen on every single hospice patient she'd ever resurrected. He was Aiden, and he had been resurrected by the man in the bed, the real Kenneth.

"It doesn't matter," she grumbled. "I'm leaving."

She tried to push past him, but he held her arm in a painful grip. "No. You aren't." He studied her for a moment. "No. We'll have ourselves a chat."

Her phone buzzed in her hand, and she lifted it to see a question emoji from Samantha. She didn't have time to respond before Kenneth—no, Aiden—grabbed the phone from her hand. This was not good.

He flipped to see the fingerprint results, and his frown deepened, before he just smiled that cold smile of his and gave her a wink. "Too clever for your own good." He pocketed her phone. "We're going for a little ride."

"The heck we are." Her heart pounded in her ears, but she knew if she ended up in a car with him, that was it for her. She couldn't pull herself out of his grip. "You got something planned, then you do it right here, Aiden."

He winced at the name, but then the cold smile returned. "No need for dramatics. I'm sure we can talk this out. Just two rational people having a discussion."

She didn't trust him, but she had little choice, given the grip he still had on her. He led her down the stairs, to a room she'd never been allowed in—his home office. The room was spartan in the extreme, but he motioned her to take one of the side chairs while he fiddled with something in a cabinet. She'd expected him to try to force her into his black SUV parked next to her Jeep. What she didn't expect was the wet cloth that came and covered her face. She fought but couldn't get loose and inhaled without thinking.

And then the world, her world, faded to black.

CHAPTER FIFTEEN

Maddy spent an unproductive day at her lab, going over reports but not really absorbing the details. When she caught herself watching the sunset outside her office window through blue-light-filtering glasses, she realized what a futile effort the day had been. She couldn't concentrate. Her emotions ran a loop between sadness and anger—sadness at losing Tamar, anger at why it happened. It all seemed ridiculous now. Sure, Tamar had some weird idea about her brothers. Well, if Maddy was honest with herself, she knew those ideas weren't new. Oh, not the body-swap thing. That was straight out of some movie script.

But even in his late teens and early twenties, Kenneth had gone through a rough period. Their parents had questioned his behavior to the point of suggesting he see a therapist. Maddy herself had seen one, but then Maddy had been a sick teen and under her parents' control. Kenneth had delayed until he reached adulthood, and then no one could force him into what he didn't want.

Maddy shook her head. Maybe Kenneth had unhealed trauma. They likely all did, but it wasn't Maddy or Tamar's job to push him on it. No. That was his business.

Yet she could disprove Tamar's other theory. A body swap could be disproved with a deep DNA analysis for twins. She puzzled that one over, staring at the equipment in her lab that could handle the job with ease. She had blood samples from both of them, but they wouldn't help, as they were current samples.

Maybe something was left at the house that would have older DNA for either of the twins. She packed up her bag with that thought and headed home as the last golden glow of sunlight across high clouds faded to full night.

She was surprised to see Kenneth's car in the driveway when she pulled up. She opened the door and called for him, but all she heard was Luis's shout of hello back down the stairs.

"Any sign of Kenneth?" she asked.

"No," Luis said. "I saw his car here when I returned from an errand about two hours ago, but not him."

Maddy frowned as she walked slowly up the stairs. She felt exhausted but determined to prove Tamar wrong. Maybe they could repair their developing relationship if they could get over this silly notion. She started out in Aiden's room, gazing down at her brother in his bed.

"Have anything left in here from the good old days?" she asked. She looked in the closet and drawers but found nothing. With a sigh, she sat at his side for a time. "Kenneth did a clean sweep of this room once you came back to us from the hospital."

A niggling thought skirted the edge of her awareness. Someone hiding who they were would clean up all old traces, wouldn't they? She stood up in a huff, angry at herself for even considering Tamar's idea. She knew it would keep worming its way through her thoughts until she nixed it with facts.

She walked into Kenneth's old room and repeated her effort. Searching the closet showed no old stuffed toys, no leftover dirty glass, or even old high school clothes that might have a stray hair or something she could use. Nothing.

She popped out of the room and came face-to-face with Kenneth.

"Looking for something?" he asked.

He looked different, more energized, but with a sheen of

sweat on his upper lip that seemed unusual for him. "Did you go for a long walk or something?" she asked.

He gave her a puzzled frown, glancing between her and his old room. "No. Jen and I went out for dinner. We took her car."

Maddy could hear the sound of someone leaving the gravel driveway. "You take advantage of that assistant of yours."

He laughed. "Always fighting for the underdog."

She followed him downstairs, noting again the extra bounce in his step and the flush in his cheeks. "You aren't dating her, are you?"

"What? No. Of course not."

Of course not, yet he showed all the signs of someone just too happy and full of life, what she'd felt she looked like before Tamar left. She brushed a stray tear out of her eye before Kenneth could see it.

"So what were you looking for in my old room?" he asked.

She couldn't tell him about Tamar's theory. "Just checking to see if there's anything hanging around we don't need anymore. There's a lot here we could donate to charity."

"Don't dump anything without asking me," he said, his hand already on the front doorknob.

"Tamar is gone," she blurted out. She didn't know why she repeated that fact to him, except she really wanted someone to talk to.

He whipped around to face her, the color fading from his cheeks. "Gone?"

"I told you she left," Maddy said.

He seemed to relax. "Well, that's good. She needed to get back to her own life at some point. Best to just leave her to it."

No. He wasn't going to be the shoulder she needed to cry on. "I'm still tutoring her for her license."

He smiled with that little wink that drove her crazy. "If she wants to continue, I'm sure she'll contact you. If she doesn't, well, you'll know the answer."

Maddy crossed her arms as he left, feeling like the only person she could talk to was the woman who'd left. She just needed to prove Tamar wrong, and then they could heal their differences. She headed to the garage and the boxes of her parents' belongings held in storage, sifting through five boxes before she found anything promising.

She opened the file with Kenneth's old high school records and memorabilia. Her parents were pack rats when it came to keeping stuff from their children's early years. She flipped through everything, but nothing struck her as useful until she found his old medical reports. She didn't think she'd discover anything useful since both brothers had the same blood type—A positive.

As she read, she paused on an older report of a skateboarding accident when Kenneth was only eight that had left him with stitches on his right big toe.

Finally. She had something. Record in hand, she locked the garage and headed back inside. She'd send a picture of this record and Aiden's toes. That would disprove Tamar's theory once and for all. She giggled at the notion of taking shots of Aiden's feet, but if it brought Tamar back into her life, it was worth it.

Tamar didn't want to wake up from her deep sleep. She'd been dreaming of kissing Maddy, and that felt like a place she wanted to stay. She tried to get back into the dream, but the straps on her arms were getting itchy.

Straps.

On her arms.

Straps.

She opened her eyes, adrenaline doing more to fight her fatigue than any sense of willpower. She tried to move but felt the restraints on her wrists and ankles. What the holy heck? Then she remembered Kenneth coming up behind her and she'd blacked out.

No. Not blacked out. He'd drugged her. And taken her where? She looked around the darkened room. It had a musty scent that matched the worn wallpaper and peeling ceiling paint she could see from the gurney she lay strapped to. She tightened her wrist to tug against the restraints, but that did nothing.

Fear grew to panic when she heard footsteps approaching. She didn't think she'd be lucky enough to have a kind stranger come find her. When the door opened behind her, she wanted to shout out anyway but kept quiet until the darkness was shattered by the flickering light of a pair of fluorescent bulbs in the ceiling.

"You're awake."

Kenneth approached from behind her. No. Not Kenneth. Aiden. Of course the jerk made her gurney face away from the only door in the room.

"Whatever you have planned, it won't help," Tamar said. "I have evidence to prove you're Aiden."

"Oh, that's not going to rescue you," he said, pulling an old metal chair closer. He popped a case onto the table next to her and clicked it open. "You see, any evidence you may have will be destroyed by the end of the night."

"You can't destroy this evidence," she said, glaring at him. "Nothing in that little kit of yours can erase your own fingerprints."

He smiled and winked. "No, but who would even think about checking fingerprints? I'm not sure how you found my juvenile record, but I'll remedy that mistake after I take care of you."

She didn't know how he'd remedy it, but it wouldn't matter. She'd sent the details to Samantha. No. What really preyed on her now was how he planned to take care of her. She didn't like what she saw coming out of his kit, but it took her a minute or two to catch on. "My blood? You're taking my blood?"

Then she realized her left arm had two restraints—one on the wrist and the other just above the elbow. She pulled against the restraints but couldn't budge her own arm, couldn't stop him from inserting the needle and attaching an empty bag to the tube. She watched that tube turn red with her own blood flowing through it.

"Why do you want my blood?"

"I'm so glad you asked. You see, your blood is even stronger than Kenneth's. Yes, you're right. I switched places with my brother. He must have pulled me out of the water after the surf accident. Of course he was so bad at swimming in the ocean, I'd already drowned by the time he rescued me. Being the angel of mercy, he of course revived me. Well, with a little help from a very confused young Maddy."

"So you paid him back by putting him in a coma?"

"Nothing so dramatic. They had both passed out when I revived. I honestly don't even know how or why. We were untrained, sure, but it shouldn't have put them both in comas."

Both? Maddy'd never said she'd ended up in that condition after the resurrection. "So why is he still in a coma but Maddy isn't?"

"Oh, that's easy. I need his blood to stay alive. Maddy's blood just isn't nearly as good."

"That's a lie. I know a necromancer doesn't keep giving blood to their resurrected."

He patted her cheek. She tried to bite him, but he pulled away too fast. "Didn't your mother teach you not to bite others?"

"Didn't yours teach you not to ruin your own brother's life after he saved yours?"

Aiden paused. "No. I don't think that came up in conversation." He smiled at her. "Parents. They never cover the important stuff, do they? And zombie research? That's nonexistent. No one tested the effects of multiple blood injections on a zombie, you see. But I did."

"You're juicing off the real Kenneth."

He laughed. "So crude, but accurate, I suppose. You see, zombies age much faster than normal. And at the age of seventeen,

I wasn't about to let myself look fifty before I hit thirty. So yes, I juiced off my brother. That, unfortunately, wasn't enough to keep him in the coma, so I sold the excess blood draws."

Jasmine was right. He was banking off necromancer blood. Now if only she were free and not in mortal danger, she could go tell the congresswoman that.

"So you plan on selling my blood."

He shook his head. "No. Yours is too precious. I plan on juicing off you as my private vintage."

Great. She had a human vampire at her elbow. Someone somewhere must be missing her by now. She just had to find ways to stall him. "And the real Kenneth?"

"Kenneth will have an unfortunate accident later. You see, you've shown me the loopholes in my body-swap game. Best for all if he's quickly cremated. It would be better for Maddy to let go of the past."

"Bullshit!" Tamar didn't flinch at her first swear in years. "Maddy loves him, even thinking he's the asshole kid you used to be. You're not killing him for her sake."

He shrugged but didn't respond before his phone rang. He turned his back to her before pulling it out of his pocket. "I'll need to take this." He stepped out of the room.

Tamar started shouting until her throat went raw, hoping someone on the other end of his call would hear her. When he walked back in with that annoying grin on his face, she knew her attempt had failed.

Before he could say anything else, a phone rang again. This time Tamar recognized her own phone's ringtone. Kenneth pulled the phone from another pocket and glared at it. "Someone named Samantha is really quite anxious to talk to you." He put the phone on the table.

"Well, I have things to attend to," he said as he disconnected the needle and held her elbow tight with gauze. "This is one pint that can go in the bank for me. Blood bank, get it?"

Did he expect her to laugh at his lame jokes?

He put a Band-Aid over where he'd drawn blood and tapped her shoulder. "One down, eight or so to go."

He walked out with a bounce to his step, a bounce he received from her blood.

Bastard.

❖

Maddy didn't have a good explanation for Luis when she stepped into Aiden's bedroom, ready to examine his toes. She could have made something up, but frankly, she didn't have the skills.

"Did you ever notice a scar on Aiden's big toe?" she asked.

Luis put down his phone. "A scar? No. Which foot?"

He stood up, pulled back the end of the covers, and peeled off blue socks to expose Aiden's feet. They were pale, like the rest of him, but she noticed how neatly trimmed his nails were. "You take good care of him."

"Thanks."

It didn't surprise her that Luis had never noticed a scar because Aiden wouldn't have one. Maddy pulled out her camera, ready to take a picture to send to Tamar and prove that Aiden was Aiden. "Can you check his right big toe?"

She clicked on her photo app and stood next to Luis, ready for her photo.

Luis lifted Aiden's right foot and leaned in closer. He lifted Aiden's big toe. "Well, shit. You're right. It's so small I never noticed it."

Maddy froze.

Luis glanced up at him. "Why'd you ask?"

She dropped the phone on the bed and picked up the exposed foot. Yes, there it was—a small scar, hardly noticeable unless she really looked up close.

A scar.

Kenneth's scar.

It was Kenneth in the bed, not Aiden. Kenneth, all these years.

Her hands trembled as she picked up her phone, again.

"Are you all right?" Luis asked as he started to cover Aiden's foot.

Not Aiden. Kenneth's foot. "Leave it exposed," she said. Not that she had a reason why, but because it reminded her of who was in the bed.

And who was living his life in Kenneth's place.

She wanted to contact Tamar and picked Tamar's number from her contacts list. The phone rang, but no one picked up. She stared down at it, wondering if she should send her a text. She sent a quick text, just a simple one.

We need to talk. Urgent.

Maddy heard the sound of a car on the gravel driveway, a car skidding to a stop right outside. She felt the jolt of fear run through her body. What if it was her brother?

"You look terrified," Luis said. "What's wrong?"

Maddy didn't realize she was holding her breath until she heard the doorbell ring and let it out with a sigh. It couldn't be Kenneth. No. She had to stop calling him that. Aiden was the conscious twin. She turned to Luis. "Can you see who that is, please?"

Clearly confused, he headed off, and within a moment, Maddy heard the click of heels on the staircase. She turned to see a tall woman with brown eyes like Tamar, but long bleached-blond hair down to her shoulders. She remembered Tamar's cousin. "Samantha." She held out her hand, but Samantha just glowered at it.

"Where is Tamar?" Samantha asked.

Maddy frowned. "She left here last night."

Luis stepped back into the room. "Well, sort of."

Both women turned to him as he explained. "She stopped by this afternoon. Said she was picking up more of her stuff." He shrugged. "I figured it was okay."

"At what time?" Samantha asked.

"Um, around two or so?"

"And you saw her leave?" Samantha asked.

"No. I went out for an errand, but her car was gone when I returned."

Maddy interrupted whatever Samantha's reply was going to be. "Sorry. Why are you here?"

Samantha glared at her, at both of them, and took a step back. "I'm leaving."

"Wait," Maddy said. "Do you think something's happened to Tamar?"

Samantha seemed to have some sort of internal debate going on. Then she took out her phone and pulled something up on it. "Before you get any bright ideas, I've already sent this to multiple people who will be calling the police if I don't report back to them every thirty minutes."

Maddy frowned. What was Samantha going on about? Maddy leaned in to scan the photo on Samantha's phone. "Sorry. What am I looking at? A set of fingerprints?"

Samantha lowered the phone. "Yes. Fingerprints that prove that man in the bed is Kenneth, not Aiden."

"Jesus," Luis said, leaning over Maddy's shoulder to look at the photos. "I knew she had doubts about Kenneth but never dreamed it was a body swap."

Maddy sank into his vacated chair. "She had the proof before I did."

Samantha glared at her. "What are you talking about?"

Maddy glanced up at her and explained why Tamar had left the night before, and what Maddy'd been doing to try to prove Tamar was wrong.

Samantha crossed her arms. "But you found out she was right. What did you do then? Cart her off for a quick burial somewhere?"

"No! God, no. I tried to call her a few minutes ago to tell her she was right."

"So this is a surprise to you?" Samantha asked, lowering her arms.

Maddy nodded. Where was Tamar if she wasn't answering even her cousin's messages? She had a sinking feeling in her gut and turned to Luis. "When did Kenneth show up?"

Samantha huffed. "You mean Aiden, don't you? Kenneth is the poor man in that bed."

Maddy closed her eyes a moment. "Yes, you're correct, but it will take me time to get used to that fact."

"Time my cousin doesn't have."

"Luis," Maddy said. "When did...my brother come today?"

Luis looked between both her and Samantha and the man in the bed. "I don't know. His car wasn't here when I went on my errand. Only Tamar's car. When I returned, her car was gone and his was here, but he wasn't. Not until he came back later while you were here."

Maddy stared at the floor. "Came back and claimed his assistant gave him a lift."

"A lie," Samantha said. "Somehow, he knows what we know and took Tamar."

Knows what we know.

Maddy stood up. "We need to leave. Luis, pack up...pack up Kenneth into the van." She turned to Samantha. "Aiden, the real Aiden is out there. He is obviously not a good man." He never was, she thought. "Our first priority is to get somewhere safe."

"That's your first priority. I need to find Tamar."

Maddy held Samantha's wrist. "We will, but we can't help each other if Aiden shows up here. First we get out, and then we figure out where Tamar is."

CHAPTER SIXTEEN

With her brother packed in the van, Maddy was about to get into the passenger seat when Samantha grabbed her arm. "I found her."

Maddy didn't quite process that statement until Samantha held up her cell phone. "We enabled tracking on each other's phones."

"Where is she?"

Samantha frowned at her phone. "Somewhere in Westborough." She looked up. "Follow me."

Maddy sat in the van and explained where they were going to Luis. He waited for Samantha to head out and then stuck to her bumper like glue as she drove along the side roads and eventually on to 495 South. Maddy watched the lights of other cars flash by, but she really wasn't seeing anything. Her mind kept replaying every instance of when Aiden, the real Aiden, had acted like himself. She and her parents had brushed it off as a psychological crutch over the loss of his brother. How could they have been so foolish? Why had it taken Tamar to see the differences, someone who barely knew them all?

And why hadn't Maddy listened to her? She couldn't stop the tears as the van sped along on the highway. If she'd listened, Tamar wouldn't be in some sort of trouble. Maddy wanted to think that her brother wouldn't harm Tamar, but what did she really know about this Aiden? He'd switched places with his brother.

She sat up straighter. "If this is Kenneth in the van, why is he still in a coma?"

Luis gave her a quick glance and returned his attention to the back of Samantha's car. "That's your specialty, not mine."

"Kenneth was the resurrector, not Aiden. So Aiden must still have been the one injured in the accident. When Kenneth and I resurrected him, I passed out." She turned to Luis. "If Kenneth passed out as well, that would have given Aiden the opportunity to switch. That still doesn't explain how and why Kenneth stayed in a coma."

Aiden had spent the entire time in the hospital with Kenneth, until he'd been brought home. "The monthly blood draws," she said. "Aiden wasn't old enough to start them right away, but I bet he snuck them out all along, until he had a legitimate reason to for his tests."

"You think those tests were real?"

Maddy sank back in her seat. "No. I think they were to keep Kenneth weak and to juice off him. It explains why neither of them showed the usual signs of accelerated aging. If Aiden was resurrected, by now he should look at least ten years older than he does."

Anger burned inside her over what he'd done. What had he been doing with her blood draws as well, and how much of that had exacerbated her own health issues? That anger fueled her all the way to Westborough.

Tamar was tired of hearing her own phone ring just out of her reach. She pulled against her restraints. She felt them hold her in place and didn't even have the satisfaction of feeling them cut into her flesh. No. These were made specifically to keep violent patients restrained without injury. She was trapped, with nothing to do but wait for Kenneth to come back and drain some more of her blood until she had nothing left. Why had he left at all instead of just draining her dry?

"Don't look a gift horse in the mouth," she grumbled to herself.

She rested a moment, staring up at the darkened ceiling because he'd turned the lights off on his way out. This was Yom Kippur. Her grandmother would be wondering where she was, maybe even worried. A tear trickled down the side of her cheek. She wouldn't see her grandmother again.

No. She couldn't give up. There had to be a way. She squirmed and pulled again and again against her restraints. Nothing budged. Nothing changed. She paused a moment before trying again.

Paused long enough to hear something in the building. Was it rats? Kenneth back already? Someone else? If there was even a glimmer of a chance some kid had wandered into this decrepit building, she had to take her chances. She shouted at the top of her lungs for help. If it was Kenneth, the worst she'd get was his smarmy smile.

Between shouts, she heard multiple footsteps. She strained to look behind her but couldn't even see the doorway into whatever room he'd tucked her into.

She couldn't see who approached but couldn't mistake the voice.

Maddy's voice.

"Here!" she shouted. "I'm in here!"

Surprise and relief flooded over her when the first person that came into view was Samantha. "Get me out of these things," she growled.

"If you'd listened to your elders and stayed away from this fucked-up family, you wouldn't be in these things," Samantha said as she fumbled with the wrist restraints.

"You're two months older than I am," Tamar said.

"And two months wiser, obviously."

Tamar's arms were free, and she had sat up to undo the restraints on her legs by the time Maddy walked into the room. Tamar watched her approach, seeing the physical strain it had taken her to get this far. She looked ready to collapse.

Tamar stood up on weak legs, not sure what to say to Maddy. Words didn't seem to be needed when Maddy wrapped her in a warm embrace.

"I'm so sorry," Maddy whispered, her breath tickling Tamar's ear.

Tamar held onto Maddy, pulling her closer. "No one could have known it would go this way."

"Um," Samantha said. "Not to break up this happy reunion, but a homicidal maniac's out there, and this is his home address right now." She waited for them to separate before adding, "No offense to you, Maddy."

"None taken, and you're right." Maddy turned to Tamar. "Kenneth, the real Kenneth, is in the van downstairs with Luis."

They headed that way, but not until Tamar grabbed the bag of her own blood. "It's not worth it to stick it back in me, but I can keep him from selling it on the black market."

She explained everything she'd learned from the real Aiden to Maddy as they made their way back out of the building, then glanced behind her once to see where her makeshift prison was. It was one of a few brick buildings with only minimal illumination from the sparse street lighting. "What is this place?"

Maddy glanced back. "Part of the old Westborough State Hospital complex, where they used to keep mental health patients around the World War Two timeframe. It's been abandoned for decades. Kenneth…Aiden talked about turning it into a necromancer training and research center but never found the state funding he needed."

"He found a use for it," Tamar mumbled.

Maddy entwined her hand in Tamar's. "Sorry."

She squeezed Maddy's hand. "Not your fault. We need to stop him, though, and I think I know how."

They paused outside Samantha's car, and everyone turned to her for an explanation.

"He's been feeding off my blood," Tamar said. "That means I have a link with him, and where there's a link, there's a way to sever it, right?"

Maddy nodded. "Of course. What you did at the vet's. It could work."

"Care to explain for those of us not playing with the dead on a regular basis?" Samantha asked, leaning against her car.

"Tamar has a unique ability that we discovered during her training. Necromancers can sever a link they have to their resurrected, but Tamar's ability goes farther than that."

Tamar grinned. "I can sever all the links to Aiden, if I can access his blood."

Samantha raised her hand. "Happy to stab him once or twice, you know, for the cause."

Maddy winced. "We won't have to do that. I still have some of his blood at my lab. Tamar and I can head there, if you'll let us use your car. You and Luis can get Kenneth to safety in the van."

Samantha tossed her keys to Tamar. "We'll be at Nanna's. If you don't show up in two hours, I'm calling the state police."

"Might need three," Tamar said. "That's a lot of driving."

Samantha glared at her and handed over Tamar's phone. "Try keeping this out of the hands of archvillains for the rest of the night?"

Tamar pocketed her phone. They had a plan, and they had the means. Time to make it happen.

❖

Tamar followed Maddy into the elevator at her lab. She felt tired but not exhausted, which meant the real Aiden hadn't used her blood recently. Maddy, on the other hand, looked beat. She leaned heavily on her cane, and while she walked with purpose, Tamar could tell this horror story had taken a deep toll on her.

She stepped up next to Maddy and offered her arm as the elevator doors opened. Maddy gave her a sad smile and took the offered assistance. The lab was dark, but rows of lights flicked on as the sensors detected them. Maddy went straight to the storage fridge in the back and unlocked the door.

"I have some of his blood stored," she said.

Tamar pulled out her bag of involuntarily donated blood. "Where should I put this?"

Maddy glanced at her over her shoulder. "There's a special drain out in the lab. Off to your right as you step outside this area."

Tamar left Maddy to find the real Aiden's blood and prepare an injector and stepped back out into the main lab. So much had changed since the first time she'd seen this place. It no longer seemed a cold, clinical area. Now it represented science and promise and Maddy, the woman she'd fallen in love with.

"Get a grip, romance girl," she said to herself and turned to her right. The special drain was clearly marked, and Tamar took her bag over there, then realized she had nothing to cut it open with. She glanced around and found a pair of scissors, then stabbed open the bag over the drain and watched it disappear. One less risk to her taken care of.

"That was an unnecessary waste."

Aiden. Tamar froze with her back still to the main lab door. She darted her glance to the locked section where Maddy was. She needed to warn her, but how?

She turned slowly around. "Aiden," she said in her loudest voice short of shouting. "You get around, don't you?"

"Not as well as you, it seems," he said. "And no need to shout. My sister knows I'm here already, don't you, Maddy?"

Tamar couldn't stop herself from glancing to her left, but she saw no sign of Maddy yet. She turned back to Aiden, the annoying smirk on his face.

"You aren't meant for intrigue, are you?" He pulled out a gun and raised his own voice. "Come on out, dear sister, or something untoward may happen to the love of your life here."

"You're a real bastard," Tamar grumbled.

"Maddy said you didn't swear," he said with a wink.

Maddy emerged from the locked room. Tamar saw no sign of the extractor. They were well and truly screwed. Samantha would call the police if she didn't hear from them soon, but that wouldn't keep the two of them alive.

Tamar stepped in front of Maddy. "It's me you want. Leave your sister out of this."

He stepped closer, the gun still pointed at her, but casually. "Oh, you made sure I couldn't, didn't you? She knows too much now. And we all understand that Kenneth was always the family favorite, wasn't he?"

"That's not true," Maddy said from behind Tamar.

Tamar sensed Maddy shift. She wanted to shout at her to lock herself back in the other room. She put her hand on Maddy's arm to keep her from moving. They paused, together, gaze locked in silent pleading.

"I'm sorry," Maddy whispered.

Tamar had less than a second to ponder what she meant before she felt the cold jab of the extractor in her palm, of all places. Then she felt Aiden's blood mix with her own. She felt the bond that linked her to him and the bonds that went to two others—Maddy and the real Kenneth.

She felt those bonds, and she severed them.

❖

Maddy held on to Tamar as she slowly collapsed to the floor.

"What did you do?" Aiden asked.

She glared at him over Tamar's shoulder as she rested the other woman in her lap. Aiden's hands shook as the gun slipped from his fingers. He clutched the edge of a lab bench.

"What did you do?" he whispered.

"What should have happened from the very beginning, Aiden. We resurrected you to give you back your life, not to let you leech off everyone else's."

He was on his knees, barely able to keep his head up to look at her. "How?"

She turned back to Tamar, who lay so still in her arms. Her soul screamed at the thought that this might have taken Tamar's life. That couldn't happen. That wouldn't happen. Maddy would inject her with her own blood if she needed to.

"How?"

She looked at her brother lying on the cold floor across from them. "She's severed all links to you. No. Don't bother talking. I wouldn't share the details with the likes of you anyway. You won't die from this, but your body swap is finished, Aiden."

Then a rush of energy returned to her. Tamar had severed whatever link remained between her and Aiden. Given her brother's unconscious body, Tamar must have successfully severed all the links. At what cost to herself, though? At what cost?

She brushed the curls from Tamar's sweaty forehead. "Come back to me," she pleaded. "Come back."

Tamar's eyes drifted open. Maddy sank into those deep-brown eyes and brushed a finger across her red lips. "You did it."

Tamar blinked, then struggled to sit up. "Man, do I feel dizzy." She looked across the floor. "Is he...?"

"Not dead," Maddy said. "And the real Kenneth should be in no worse condition either. If it's anything like I feel, he should be better."

"Better," Tamar repeated. She looked back at Maddy. "Thanks for the jab, but for future reference, getting it in the palm really, really hurts."

Maddy chuckled, then leaned over and pulled Tamar's face closer. "Let's hope there's no need for future references to this scenario."

Tamar nodded as her gaze drifted down to Maddy's lips. Maddy took the hint and pressed her lips to Tamar's.

She had likely lost her brother to prison for a time, but she'd gained someone so precious to her—a lifelong partner.

CHAPTER SEVENTEEN

Tamar poured another bowl of her grandmother's homemade chicken soup and carried it into the living room. Kenneth, the real Kenneth, sat propped up on pillows on the sofa with Kalev draped across his feet, keeping a close eye on the tortoise Kenneth fed a bit of lettuce to on his lap. Kenneth remained weak, but after he woke from the coma and a long stint in rehab, he was finally able to get around some with the assistance of Maddy's old walker. And after he woke up the first time in her grandmother's house, Nanna had all but adopted him as her own.

"Here you go," Tamar said, handing him the bowl.

"You know," he said. "I don't come here to be fed all the time."

"Of course not," Nanna said. "You come here for the philosophical debates. You stay for the soup."

He laughed and saluted her with his spoon.

Maddy pulled Tamar down onto the loveseat next to her and kissed her cheek. "We all stay for the soup."

"Not me," Samantha said, emerging from the kitchen. "I've had my fill of chicken soup for the next year. And I need to get back to civilization. You bohemians enjoy yourselves." She hugged their grandmother and smacked Tamar on the back of the head for good measure.

"Hey, what's that for?" Tamar asked.

"Just paying it forward for the next time you drag us all into some wacked-out necromancy scheme."

Tamar smiled. "Not me."

"Right," Samantha said. "Not you, who just framed her official license and who is now a part-time consultant to the acting necromancer marshal for the state."

"Who'd have thought Jasmine Bunte would nominate me for that position?" Maddy squeezed Tamar's hand. "I'd hire Tamar full-time if she let me."

"Well, I do want to keep some of my old life intact," Tamar said.

"We'll see how long that lasts." Samantha waved them good-bye at the door.

Tamar glanced down at her and Maddy's entwined hands, with their matching gold and silver engagement rings. So much had changed for her this year. The real Aiden was in prison awaiting trial and was already showing signs of rapid aging now that he had no necromancy links to the rest of them. She glanced up at Kenneth, who had already begun his usual philosophical discussions with her grandmother.

So much had changed for all of them.

She leaned near and kissed Maddy.

"What's that for?" Maddy asked.

"For you. And for us."

For their future.

About the Author

Sandra Barret is a native New Englander who wanted to be an archaeologist. So of course she ended up a writer for a software company. She focuses her fiction writing on urban fantasy and science fiction stories where strong women save the day. When not writing, she's reading, gardening, and occasionally digging holes way too deep in the back of her historic home in the hopes of finding something more archaeologically significant than the ever-present coal slag. Dreams never die, they just adapt to life circumstances!

Books Available From Bold Strokes Books

Coasting and Crashing by Ana Hartnett. Life comes easy to Emma Wilson until Lake Palmer shows up at Alder University and derails her every plan. (978-1-63679-511-9)

Every Beat of Her Heart by KC Richardson. Piper and Gillian have their own fears about falling in love, but will they be able to overcome those feelings once they learn each other's secrets? (978-1-63679-515-7)

Fire in the Sky by Radclyffe and Julie Cannon. Two women from different worlds have nothing in common and every reason to wish they'd never met—except for the attraction neither can deny. (978-1-63679-561-4)

Grave Consequences by Sandra Barret. A decade after necromancy became licensed and legalized, can Tamar and Maddy overcome the lingering prejudice against their kind and their growing attraction to each other to uncover a plot that threatens both their lives? (978-1-63679-467-9)

Haunted by Myth by Barbara Ann Wright. When ghost-hunter Chloe seeks an answer to the current spectral epidemic, all clues point to one very famous face: Helen of Troy, whose motives are more complicated than history suggests and whose charms few can resist. (978-1-63679-461-7)

Invisible by Anna Larner. When medical school dropout Phoebe Frink falls for the shy costume shop assistant Violet Unwin, everything about their love feels certain, but can the same be said about their future? (978-1-63679-469-3)

Like They Do in the Movies by Nan Campbell. Celebrity gossip writer Fran Underhill becomes Chelsea Cartwright's personal assistant with the aim of taking the popular actress down, but neither of them anticipates the clash of their attraction. (978-1-63679-525-6)

Limelight by Gun Brooke. Liberty Bell and Palmer Elliston loathe each other. They clash every week on the hottest new TV show, until Liberty starts to sing and the impossible happens. (978-1-63679-192-0)

Playing with Matches by Georgia Beers. To help save Cori's store and help Liz survive her ex's wedding, they strike a deal: a fake relationship, but just for one week. There's no way this will turn into the real deal. (978-1-63679-507-2)

The Memories of Marlie Rose by Morgan Lee Miller. Broadway legend Marlie Rose undergoes a procedure to erase all of her unwanted memories, but as she starts regretting her decision, she discovers that the only person who could help is the love she's trying to forget. (978-1-63679-347-4)

The Murders at Sugar Mill Farm by Ronica Black. A serial killer is on the loose in southern Louisiana, and it's up to three women to solve the case while carefully dancing around feelings for each other. (978-1-63679-455-6)

A Talent Ignited by Suzanne Lenoir. When Evelyne is abducted and Annika believes she has been abandoned, they must risk everything to find each other again. (978-1-63679-483-9)

All Things Beautiful by Alaina Erdell. Casey Norford only planned to learn to paint like her mentor, Leighton Vaughn, not sleep with her. (978-1-63679-479-2)

An Atlas to Forever by Krystina Rivers. Can Atlas, a difficult dog Ellie inherits after the death of her best friend, help the busy hopeless romantic find forever love with commitment-phobic animal behaviorist Hayden Brandt? (978-1-63679-451-8)

Bait and Witch by Clifford Mae Henderson. When Zeddi gets an unexpected inheritance from her client Mags, she discovers that Mags served as high priestess to a dwindling coven of old witches—who are positive that Mags was murdered. Zeddi owes it to her to uncover the truth. (978-1-63679-535-5)

Buried Secrets by Sheri Lewis Wohl. Tuesday and Addie, along with Tuesday's dog, Tripper, struggle to solve a twenty-five-year-old mystery while searching for love and redemption along the way. (978-1-63679-396-2)

Come Find Me in the Midnight Sun by Bailey Bridgewater. In Alaska, disappearing is the easy part. When two men go missing, state trooper Louisa Linebach must solve the case, and when she thinks she's coming close, she's wrong. (978-1-63679-566-9)

Death on the Water by CJ Birch. The Ocean Summit's authorities have ruled a death on board its inaugural cruise as a suicide, but Claire suspects murder, and with the help of Assistant Cruise Director Moira, Claire conducts her own investigation. (978-1-63679-497-6)

Living For You by Jenny Frame. Can Sera Debrek face real and personal demons to help save the world from darkness and open her heart to love? (978-1-63679-491-4)

Ride with Me by Jenna Jarvis. When Lucy's vacation to find herself becomes Emma's chance to remember herself, they realize that everything they're looking for might already be sitting right next to them—if they're willing to reach for it. (978-1-63679-499-0)

Rivals for Love by Ali Vali. Brooks Boseman's brother Curtis is getting married, and Brooks needs to be at the engagement party. Only she can't possibly go, not with Curtis set to marry the secret love of her youth, Fallon Goodwin. (978-1-63679-384-9)

Whiskey and Wine by Kelly and Tana Fireside. Winemaker Tessa Williams and sex toy shop owner Lace Reynolds are both used to taking risks, but will they be willing to put their friendship on the line if it gives them a shot at finding forever love? (978-1-63679-531-7)

Hands of the Morri by Heather K O'Malley. Discovering she is a Lost Sister and growing acquainted with her new body, Asche learns how to be a warrior and commune with the Goddess the Hands serve, the Morri. (978-1-63679-465-5)

I Know About You by Erin Kaste. With her stalker inching closer to the truth, Cary Smith is forced to face the past she's tried desperately to forget. (978-1-63679-513-3)

Mate of Her Own by Elena Abbott. When Heather McKenna finally confronts the family who cursed her, her werewolf is shocked to discover her one true mate, and that's only the beginning. (978-1-63679-481-5)

Pumpkin Spice by Tagan Shepard. For Nicki, new love is making this pumpkin spice season sweeter than expected. (978-1-63679-388-7)

Sweat Equity by Aurora Rey. When cheesemaker Sy Travino takes a job in rural Vermont and hires contractor Maddie Barrow to rehab a house she buys sight unseen, they both wind up with a lot more than they bargained for. (978-1-63679-487-7)

Taking the Plunge by Amanda Radley. When Regina Avery meets model Grace Holland—the most beautiful woman she's ever seen—she doesn't have a clue how to flirt, date, or hold on to a relationship. But Regina must take the plunge with Grace and hope she manages to swim. (978-1-63679-400-6)

We Met in a Bar by Claire Forsythe. Wealthy nightclub owner Erica turns undercover bartender on a mission to catch a thief where she meets no-strings, no-commitments Charlie, who couldn't be further from Erica's type. Right? (978-1-63679-521-8)

Western Blue by Suzie Clarke. Step back in time to this historic western filled with heroism, loyalty, friendship, and love. The odds are against this unlikely group—but never underestimate women who have nothing to lose. (978-1-63679-095-4)

Windswept by Patricia Evans. The windswept shores of the Scottish Highlands weave magic for two people convinced they'd never fall in love again. (978-1-63679-382-5)

A Calculated Risk by Cari Hunter. Detective Jo Shaw doesn't need complications, but the stabbing of a young woman brings plenty of those, and Jo will have to risk everything if she's going to make it through the case alive. (978-1-63679-477-8)

An Independent Woman by Kit Meredith. Alex and Rebecca's attraction won't stop smoldering, despite their reluctance to act on it and incompatible poly relationship styles. (978-1-63679-553-9)

Cherish by Kris Bryant. Josie and Olivia cherish the time spent together, but when the summer ends and their temporary romance melts into the real deal, reality gets complicated. (978-1-63679-567-6)

Cold Case Heat by Mary P. Burns. Sydney Hansen receives a threat in a very cold murder case that sends her to the police for help, where she finds more than justice with Detective Gale Sterling. (978-1-63679-374-0)